Good Girl
WITH A
DOPE BOY
Fetish
2

A NOVEL BY

PORSCHEA JADE

© 2017

Published by Royalty Publishing House
www.royaltypublishinghouse.com

PREVIOUSLY

Myeke

After hanging up the phone with O'Hajee, I had been pacing the floor waiting for the little nigga to walk through the door. Something about his voice scared me. He sounded like he was about to cry, and that shit sent my mind into overdrive. I had seen O'Hajee cry twice my whole life, and that was when our older brother Rod died, and when he got sick and couldn't make his basketball tournament. That little nigga's soul was crushed. He swore he was going to be the next Kobe, and he could've been had he not quit school.

Hearing the front door open and close, I stopped pacing, expecting O'Hajee to walk around the corner, but it wasn't him; it was Al.

"My bad, boss man. I been tryin' to get you on your phone and you wasn't answerin', so I just popped up," he explained.

"It's cool. I haven't looked at it since I talked to Hajee about an hour ago," I told him.

"Speaking of Hajee…" he started, but his voice trailed off.

"Where my lil' brother at, Al? He good?" I questioned.

"I'on know what's goin' on, Key. I just know what Ant told me. He sent me some stuff, and he was gon' come by and tell you, but I told him not to and to let me handle it before you body the lil' nigga."

"You ain't makin' no sense, Al. If you got somethin' to say, spit the shit out, my nigga," I snapped.

"Ant saw Hajee in Philly."

"Okay, so. Motherfuckas be in Philly every day, B. What the fuck that got to do wit' anything?" I shrugged, pacing the floor again.

"Nah, you ain't understandin', Key. He saw Hajee in Philly at Deuce's crib," Al said, causing me to stop moving.

"Say that shit again."

"He saw him, Key, and any other time, I would've thought the lil' nigga was trippin', but he got pictures—"

"What pictures?" I asked, cutting him off.

"He sent them to you."

Before he could say anything else, I walked over to the coffee table beside my couch and snatched up my phone. Unlocking it, I scrolled through to my messages and, sure enough, he had sent me five pictures and called me half a dozen times since I had talked to Hajee an hour ago.

Opening up the pictures, my blood pressure started going through the roof as I saw pictures of O'Hajee getting out of his car and knocking on the door, and pictures of his car, and of him leaving.

What the fuck was he doing wit' that nigga, Sac? I thought, scrolling through the pictures.

"And there's something else, Key—" But before he could finish his sentence, I snatched up my truck keys and started stomping out of the living room, headed to my truck.

"I'ma kill that lil' nigga!" I seethed through gritted teeth.

"Boss man, I think you need to talk to him," Al said, coming up behind me as I unlocked the door.

"Well too damn bad I'on give a fuck about what you think right now, my nigga," I snapped, and got into the driver's seat before he could say another word. I hopped in the truck and did a dash all the way to the highway.

If he was in Philly when he called me, I should still beat his ass to mom's and planned to be there when that lil' nigga got there. Cutting my drive-in half, I pulled into the parking lot on two wheels and almost hit some nigga standing in a parking spot, I was driving so damn fast.

Killing the engine, I locked my car and jogged the distance to the doors and took the stairs three at a time. Busting in the apartment, I walked past my mom without speaking and went straight towards O'Hajee's room.

"Excuse you! I know I'm not fucking invisible!" my mom yelled from the living room.

Pushing open Hajee's door, I hit it so hard that it smacked the wall, and I know that the knob probably left a dent. I didn't give a fuck; I would pay for the shit anyway.

"Why the hell are you walking around my damn house like you

don't have any damn since, Myeke?"

"Where's your son?" I snapped, ignoring her question.

"My son? Well my son happens to be your little brother, or did you forget that?" she asked, folding her arms over her chest.

"Nah, that lil' nigga ain't shit to me, and when I get my hands on his ass, I'ma push that nigga's shit back. I can handle betrayal from everyone else, but not that nigga!" I yelled, punching a hole in the wall.

"You have thirty seconds to calm the hell down and tell me what the hell is going on, or I'm goin' to forget you are my son and punch ya disrespectful ass in the face."

Grilling her, I stared at her and plopped down on O'Hajee's bed and ran my fingers through my hair. I was getting a headache, and if I didn't calm down soon, I was going to fuck around and make myself pass out from high blood pressure.

"I got robbed by a nigga a couple weeks back, and one of my runners just saw Hajee out at the nigga's house," I admitted.

Sitting down next to me, she rubbed my back, trying to calm me down like she did when I was a kid and got too upset.

"I'm sure there's a good explanation, Myeke. You gotta give him a chance to explain. It may not be what you think."

Blowing out a breath of frustration, I ran a hand down my face and prepared to reply to what she said when something caught my eye. There were blood spots next to O'Hajee's closet and the door was cracked.

Standing to my feet, I walked over to the closet and opened it, and guess what the fuck I saw? His backpack full of my drugs. I knew my dope from anywhere in the world. My connect put scorpions on all his packaging. Bending down, I grabbed the bag and realized that it was covered in blood and there was a pair of clothes with blood spots on them.

Standing to my feet, I spun around to look at my mom and shook my head.

"Innocent, huh? When was he here, Ma?" I asked, stepping closer to her.

"Now, Myeke—"

"MA! WHEN WAS HE HERE!" I bellowed.

I hated raising my voice at her, but the way I saw it, she was just as guilty as him for trying to protect him like she didn't know what the fuck was going on.

"He left here ten minutes ago, Myeke! He's scared about something. You need to go find your brother," she stressed, walking towards me.

"Oh, trust me, I plan to," I seethed, brushing past her and walking out the room and out the front door.

Pulling out my phone, I sent him a text to let him know I was coming to find him, and he'd better say his prayers before I got there.

I could hear my mom screaming my name from the door, but I wasn't trying to hear shit else that she had to say. The only thing that was saving O'Hajee right now was the fact that I didn't want my mom to be down two sons, but at the same time, if he said some shit that I didn't like, I was going to split his shit and pray that my mom found it in her heart to forgive me one day.

As I got in the truck, headed back to my house, my phone started ringing. Checking the screen, I saw that it was Siya and hit the decline button. I hadn't spoken to her ass since I had to yoke her up at the house, and I didn't plan on talking to her any time soon. The less drama tonight, the better.

Calling back almost immediately, I pressed the ignore button at least three more times on her before I finally gave in and answered the phone.

"What the fuck do you want, A'Siya!" I snapped into the phone.

"Key. It's Karson," she cried. "I don't know what's wrong wit' him. He's breathing funny."

Feeling my heart drop to the pit of my stomach, I temporarily lost hearing as I thought about something being wrong with my son.

"What hospital you taking him to? I'm on my way," I said, busting a U-Turn in the middle of the road.

"No! I don't have my car. We're at Mom's. You gotta come get us!" she cried.

"What the hell is wrong wit' your car, Sy?"

"I got a flat! Hurry, Key. I'm scared, and his breathing is getting worse."

"Calm down, I'm on my way! I'm ten minutes away. I'll call you as soon as I turn on your mom's block so that you can bring him outside," I told her, hanging up in her ear.

Pushing my foot down on the gas pedal, I sped all the way down the block trying to get to my son and his mother. Within eight minutes, I was turning on her mom's block. Dialing her number, she picked up just as I pulled into the yard.

"I'm outside!" I yelled, throwing the car in park.

"I'm sorry, Key. I love you," Siya said in a low tone.

All the hint of crying was gone out of her voice, and I instantly got worried.

"What are you talkin' about, Siya? Where's my son?" I asked, preparing to get out of the car.

"Look up," she said before the line went dead.

Looking toward the house, for the first time I noticed that her car was nowhere to be seen, and there was someone standing on the passenger side of my car and another in the front.

It seemed like everything moved in slow motion as I watched the shooters aiming their guns at me.

"Dirty bitch," was the last thing I could say before gunshots broke out.

Rat! Tat! Tat! Tat!

Rat! Tat! Tat! Tat!

Zoie

I counted out fifty minutes in my head before pulling my body off the blood and cum soaked mattress. Walking was painful, but nothing could make me stay in this house a minute longer. I was afraid that they would come back for a round twelve, and I knew that I wouldn't be able to live through that again.

Dragging my body to the door, I walked out of it and limped to the staircase. I don't know what made me want him so bad, but I needed him. I didn't care why he cut me off. I didn't care what he did; I just needed him.

What should have taken me less than two minutes, took me close to twenty, as I dragged myself up the flight of stairs, fighting hard to fight the dark cloud that was trying to take over me. I finally made it to O'Hajee's front door.

Instinctively, I twisted the knob and the door opened right on up, and I used all the energy I could muster to stumble down the hallway headed towards his bedroom.

My ears started ringing, and I began to black out, and I could swear that my ears were replaying the scene of what happened over and over again. I could hear a male moaning as I put my hand on O'Hajee's room door. Leaning my body against the door, I twisted the knob and almost fell as the door opened up.

Dropping to my knees, tears clouded my vision as I watched O'Hajee shove his dick in and out of the girl Monica that I fought a few weeks back.

"Yo, what the fuck!" He spun around with anger etched on his face until he realized who it was.

"Zoie? Baby! Zoie!" I heard him call me.

Just as my body started to collapse, he reached me just before I hit the ground and cradled me in his arms with tears in his eyes.

"Zoie, say something, ma!" he cried out. "What the fuck you just sittin' there lookin' dumb for! Call the fuckin' ambulance!" he barked at Monica.

With shaky hands, I reached up and wiped a tear that was leaking down his face. I could see the hurt in his eyes as I tried to focus on him and tell him that I was okay, but I could feel the sleep trying to take over me as my body began to shake violently and my eyes rolled into the back of my head.

"Zoie! Open your eyes! Zoie!" was the last thing I heard him scream before the dark cloud I had been fighting finally won the battle, and I lost consciousness.

CHAPTER ONE

O'Hajee

Thirty-seven stitches.

Thirty-seven stitches, is what they told me it would take to repair the tearing and damage caused to her. Thirty-seven exactly. She would need fifteen to close the gashes on her body, and she needed a blood transfusion. I had been sitting in the waiting room for an hour, and the doctor had just come out and told me all this. It sounded like I was underwater as I listened to her explain that Zoie's body went into shock twice and caused her heart to start failing from all the stress.

Not my girl. Not my lil' mamas, I thought as tears leaked from my eyes.

No one was here for her but me. I guess my mom was right; I was all she had, and I pushed her away when she needed me most. I couldn't get in touch with Myeke to save my life. I understood that he was mad at me, but I needed him. I needed him more than ever because, for once, I was lost and didn't have any answers to the questions they asked.

The sound of feet coming toward me caused my head to shoot

up as I watched Al charging at me like a pissed off bull. Just as I stood to my feet, the nigga wrapped his hand around my throat and started to squeeze so hard I thought my eyes would pop out of my head.

"After all that nigga's done for you, you would snake him, my nigga? Over some pussy ass nigga that wasn't your own!" Al gritted.

I couldn't respond if I wanted to; the nigga was cutting off my air supply, and I was starting to get light-headed.

"That's enough, Alphonse!" I faintly heard my mom shout before he dropped my body.

Going into a coughing fit, I instinctively started rubbing my neck to ease the pain and tried to catch my breath.

"What the fuck is wrong wit' you, son? I know the nigga ain't speakin' to me, but he really sent you to murk me?" I asked in a raspy voice.

"What the fuck is wrong wit' me, my nigga? You would ask me that shit after the shit you did! You the one sitting in the hospital wit' blood soakin' ya clothes! You could've at least had the decency to wipe your brother's blood off you before you tried to come up here and act like the grieving brother, B!" Al shouted, and I swear all the wind left my lungs.

My brother's blood.

"What the fuck you talkin' 'bout, Al?"

"You know exactly what the fuck I'm talkin' about, lil' nigga. The evidence all over your body," he shot back with a grimace on his face.

"THIS IS ZOIE'S BLOOD!" I snapped. "NOW, WHAT THE

FUCK HAPPENED TO MY BROTHER!"

I was so loud that everyone that was paying attention to us jumped in their seats and tried to move out of the way before something bad happened.

Giving me the once over again, his face started to soften as he thought about what I had just said, but fuck that, I didn't need his sympathy. All I wanted to know was where my brother was.

"Zoie? What happened to Zoie?" My mother panicked, and for the first time, I noticed that she had been crying.

"We'll talk 'bout that shit later, Ma. Please. Just tell me what happened."

"Your brother came to the house looking for you. He was shouting about how he was going to kill you when he got ahold of you. Last thing I heard was that he was headed home to find you because you were supposed to meet him at his house. I got a call about two hours ago from the hospital saying someone found his body at the emergency room entrance," she explained, and I felt my mouth go dry. "They shot him, Hajee. They shot my baby." She cried and broke down in my arms.

"Who did this?" I asked, cutting my eyes over at Al.

"I should be askin' you that, my nigga. From where I stand, you the only one that had it in you to do it. You got the most to lose now that Key knows the truth."

"WHY THE FUCK WOULD I TRY TO KILL MY BROTHER, MY NIGGA? HUH? ANSWER ME THAT! IF I WANTED THAT NIGGA DEAD, THEN TRUST THAT HE WOULD BE!"

"Excuse me. If you don't calm down, I'm going to have to ask you to leave," I heard a woman's voice say.

Looking over my shoulder, I realized it was Zoie's doctor, and I turned around temporarily forgetting what had just happened.

"How is she, Doc? Is she okay? How did the blood thing go?" I was firing off questions left and right.

"Ms. Neal is fine. We had to sedate her after we gave her the blood because she woke up kicking and screaming. We're going to have to monitor her for the next few hours to see how her body reacts to the new blood, and then once we know for sure, we're going to move her into protective custody. Whoever did this to her is still out there and very dangerous. We pulled three DNA samples from her skin, clothes, vaginal canal, and rectum.

It's standard after a rape, especially one as severe as this one, to treat for any diseases that may have happened. Until I know more, since you brought her here, you are the only one able to visit. We need to do everything we can to prevent this from happening again or causing her stress. Her heart is still in bad shape, and stress will slow down her healing process," she explained, and I could feel tears stinging my eyes again.

"Three? So you mean to tell me that three niggas raped my girl?"

"Yes, that's what it looks like. We've sent the samples to be tested to see if we get a DNA hit. I'm so sorry, Mr. Compton, but as soon as she's able to have visitors, I will come find you. I promise. You have a tough one," she said, patting me on the arm. "I must go. I was on my way to look for another family," she told me before walking a few feet away and looking down at the chart in her hand.

"Family of Myeke Compton!" she shouted.

"Right here, Doc," I spoke up, and she looked back at me with a shocked look.

"Looks like your two to none tonight, huh?"

I tried to give her a small smile, but I know it looked more awkward than anything.

"Who is Mr. Compton to you?" she asked, looking over his chart.

"His brother. I'm his mother, and this is my godson," my mom said, introducing everyone. "How is he?"

"Mr. Compton sustained several bullets that entered his body. Most exited the body, but one in particular hit his spleen, and we had to remove it. Without a spleen, Myeke will be more prone to infection but can live without it. There were a total of eleven bullet wounds. He did lose a lot of blood, but whoever brought him here did so just in time, or we wouldn't be having this conversation now.

Due to the extent of his injuries, we placed him in a medically induced coma so that his body can begin the healing process. Over the next few weeks, we will slowly wean him off the drugs once we feel that he is out of the woods. His condition is critical, but something is telling me that he's not going out without a fight," she explained.

I couldn't win for losing today. Like, what the fuck was it? A fucking full moon? After thanking the doctor again, I went back to my original spot I had been in and got comfortable. I wasn't leaving this hospital until I saw both my brother and my girl.

Yep, it's gon' be a long night, I thought, sitting back in my seat.

A'Siya

Banging my hands on the steering wheel, I looked over in the passenger seat that was soaked in blood. The sound of gunshots going off still rang in my ears, as I drove with no clear destination in mind. I tried to blink back the tears that filled my eyes as everything that transpired tonight replayed in my mind. I sat down the block from my mom's house and watched the man I loved be shot like he was hunted for sport, and in that moment, I knew then that my life would never be the same, and it was all my fault.

My decision to set him up was selfish, and I was now headed far, far away, where he would never find me, but as I watched him fall out of his truck, soaked in blood, something shifted inside me, and I couldn't let him bleed out in the street like roadkill. I prayed the whole way to the hospital as he floated in and out of consciousness.

I wasn't even a religious person, but I couldn't allow him to die because of my own personal gain. I was still going to take his money and get the fuck out of dodge, but that didn't mean I wanted him dead. Down the block from the emergency room entrance, I pulled a black hoodie over my head and made sure that no hair was showing before pulling the drawstrings tight over my face. I already knew the first thing they would check for is the cameras when they discovered his body.

Pulling up to the entrance, it took all the strength I had in my body to pull his body out of the car and lay him on the ground, before running to the other side and pressing my horn for thirty seconds flat and burning off into the night. I just prayed that they could save him in time. I may not have wanted to be with him anymore, but Karson deserved to at least know that his father was still alive, even if he could never see him again.

Hopping on the interstate, I headed for the one place that I didn't think anyone would look for me. I just prayed that she opened the door when I got there.

* * * *

Fifteen hours later, I was down south looking like a fish out of water. I swear Atlanta had to be one of the biggest cities in the south, but it was country as fuck. These dudes down here talked like they were slow, and none of these motherfuckas could drive if their life depended on it. Shit was mad annoying, but beggars couldn't be choosy.

Putting the car in park, I looked over my appearance, trying to straighten up as best as I could before I got out of the car and walked up to the house and rang the doorbell. Looking over my shoulder, I bounced from one foot to the other and rang the doorbell again.

"Who is it!" I heard a deep voice shout from the other side.

Furrowing my eyebrows in confusion, I knocked on the door with the little strength I had in my body. I must've had the wrong address, but I needed confirmation.

"Bruh, who the fuck is it!" the voice snapped before the door flew open, and I came face to face with a chocolate god.

This nigga was everything, and I swear I felt that familiar tingle in my panties as my lips puckered at the scowl that he had etched on his face. This man was fine as hell, and I swear that I couldn't do shit but stare. I almost forgot why I was standing here as I openly eye fucked him.

"Look, we don't want whatever it is that you're selling. We ain't wit' that bumming shit. They got plenty of shelters around this motherfucka that help the homeless. Gon' get you some help, shorty." He damn near growled at me with a look of disgust on his face, taking in my appearance.

Damn, I knew I looked fucked up, but I know this bitch ass nigga didn't just call me homeless.

"Homeless? Bum ass nigga, fuck outta here! You don't fuckin' know me, but I guarantee that I got more money in my pockets than you've ever fuckin' seen in ya bitch ass life!" I clapped back.

Who the fuck did this nigga think he was? I didn't give a fuck how fine he was, if a motherfucka came at my neck, I was coming for their heart. Fuck I look like? Ol' corny ass nigga.

"What the hell is all this fuckin' noise!" I heard the voice I had been looking for.

Within seconds, she came into view, pushing his ass out the way with a mean mug on her face. When she noticed it was me that he was arguing with, her face went from angry to confused.

"Siya? What the hell are you doin' here?"

"Damn, Syd. Is that how you talk to your big sister? You not happy to see me?" I asked with a slight smirk on my face.

"Sydney, you know this broad?" the dude asked.

"Yeah, baby. This is my sister I was telling you about. This is A'Siya," she replied, introducing us. "Go ahead in the back. I'll handle this, baby," she told him, soothingly rubbing his arm.

Without another word, he gave me another once over before shaking his head and retreating to the back of the house. She followed him with her eyes until she couldn't see him anymore, before turning back to me.

"What's goin' on, Sy? I haven't heard from you in damn near four years. Now you just show up on my doorstep uninvited, looking like you been in a fight with Mayweather. Is that blood?" Syd asked, taking in my appearance.

Okay, here goes nothing.

Putting my head down, my shoulders started to shake slightly as I moved my head from side to side.

"Siya? What's wrong?"

"They shot him, Syd. Myeke. He was coming to meet me at Mom's to pick me and Karson up for dinner, and I guess some guys must've followed him. It was so loud and there was so much blood," I cried.

I was crying so hard, you would think that my tears were real. We grew up in the hood, so hearing gunshots wasn't nothing new, but I had to sell this. I needed her more than ever, especially since Deuce's dumb ass wasn't picking up his phone.

"Damn, Sy! Dead ass?"

Nodding my head up and down fast, my lips trembled, and I tried to put together some words, but I couldn't.

"I don't think he made it. There was so much blood when I got him to the hospital. I couldn't stay there. What if they came back? How was I going to protect Karson?" I sobbed.

"Shhhhh," she whispered, pulling me into her arms and rocking me gently. "Nothing's going to happen to you or Karson. Where is he now?"

"In the back seat, sleeping. He doesn't know what happened. I packed up as much stuff as I could and came straight here. I didn't know what else to do."

"Well, let's go get my nephew and we'll sort this out later. Let's just get you cleaned up," she told me. "Babe!" she turned around and shouted.

"Yeah?" the dude said, coming back around the corner.

"Can you go get their bags and bring them inside while I show Siya where her and Karson gon' be sleeping?"

"Wait, they stayin' here?" he questioned as his eyebrows dipped at the idea.

"Nigga, now ain't the time to be askin' questions, Marcus, damn! Please, just go get the bags. You gettin' me tight, and I swear I'll send your ass back to ya fuckin' house if it's a problem. Fuck outta here!" Syd snapped at him, and I smiled internally.

Guess being in the south didn't take the spunk away from my sister. Shit, it ain't nothing like a Philly bitch.

"Chill out wit' all that!" he told her, shaking his head.

"Then stop bein' a fuckin' goof and go get the shit," she retorted. "C'mon, Sy."

"Oh yeah," I started to say to him. "My son is in the back seat, sleeping. If you nudge him, he can walk inside by himself," I told him.

Instead of responding to what I said, he grilled my ass and kept walking. I didn't give a fuck about him being tight; the nigga was just going to have to deal with it.

After Syd showed me the guest bedroom, Marcus came in and set our stuff down without a word while I heard Syd talking to Karson, and he was asking her a million and two questions. Going in the bathroom, I stripped out of my bloody clothes and got in the shower under the warm water. I watched as the blood mixed in with the water and went down the drain.

Okay, Siya. You accomplished step one. Now, let's find a way to finish part two, I thought to myself as I let the water run over my body.

I could tell now that Marcus was going to be a problem with me getting closer to Sydney, but I wasn't worried about that. If he became too much of an issue, it was nothing to add his ass to the list of motherfuckas that crossed me and didn't live to tell the story. I had an agenda to uphold, and anyone that got in the way could get it. Even that nigga.

CHAPTER TWO

Zoie

A week later.

Beep.

Beep.

Beep.

The constant noise was bothering me as I tried to sleep in the bed. A pain shot through my chest as I tried to move. Rolling over, I got tangled up in something and opened my eyes to see that I wasn't in my bed or O'Hajee's. Jumping up, my head started to spin, and the beeping noise started going crazy.

Looking around the room, I noticed that it was dark, and I could see a body lying in a chair on the opposite side of the room. I guess the beeping started to bother them because they stretched their body and looked in my direction. Noticing I was sitting up, the person jumped to their feet and came over to me.

"Zoie," the voice called out to me, and it was like music to my ears.

It was O'Hajee.

"Baby! You're awake. Let me go get the nurse. Don't move," he said so fast that he didn't even come to me fully before running out of the room.

Hearing the word nurse, I looked around the room again and noticed that I was in a hospital bed.

Why am I in the hospital? I thought to myself.

A minute later, the room door swung open, and O'Hajee came in, followed by a woman dressed in scrubs and another woman in a lab coat, turning on the room light. I squinted my eyes so they could adjust to them.

"Ms. Neal, I'm glad to see that you're awake. It's been a very long week. My name is Dr. Emily James, but you can call me Em," she greeted. "How are you feeling?"

"A week?" I croaked. "Why am I here?"

My throat felt like sandpaper, and I rubbed it to relieve some of the pain.

"Let me get you some water," the nurse said.

Stopping for a second, she poured me a cup of ice water and handed it to me before she started working on my vitals.

"What is the last thing you remember?" Em asked, looking at me.

Giving her a confused look, I looked over at O'Hajee, whose face held so much pain that my eyebrows dipped further. Trying to think back to the last thing I remembered, I ran through the last events in my head, trying to figure out what I was doing before I fell asleep.

Blood. A lot of blood. My mom… and Mike. As everything started to come back to me, my heart started to beat fast and I started to hyperventilate. I couldn't breathe. Closing my eyes tightly, I shook my head from side to side, trying to erase the images in my mind. I could feel their hands on my body. And the feel of them shoving themselves in me.

I could feel the tight grip on my arms and I could hear myself screaming. Begging. Crying to my mother for her not to let them do this to me.

"Ms. Neal? Ms. Neal! Please calm down. You're getting yourself worked up," the doctor said, and I opened my eyes again with tears running down my cheeks.

"I remember," I whispered.

"Can you tell me who did this to you?" she asked.

Shaking my head from side to side, I didn't know their names. I could barely remember their faces. I just remembered their voices. I couldn't tell them who did this to me. The pain and sorrow I was feeling for myself was turning into hate as I thought about my mother and Mike. I didn't want the hospital to handle it. This was something I had to do.

"I don't know. It was dark," I told her, dropping my head.

"From what we picked up off your body, there were a total of three DNA samples on you, as well as severe bruising and opened cuts on your body. The pain caused your body to go into shock. If it wasn't for Mr. Compton, you may not have made it," she told me, and I looked up at him with a blank expression on my face.

I remembered everything alright. I didn't know how I got here, but I do remember going to his house and seeing him... with her.

Not bothering to show any emotion, I looked back at the doctor and waited on the nurse to finish checking me out and attempt to calm my heart rate down.

"With your body going into shock, it caused some heart failure. We had to put you in a temporary coma to allow your body to heal some. It's only been a week, so the bruising is still there, and your stitches will continue to dissolve for another two weeks or so."

"Stitches?" I gasped.

"Yes, ma'am. The tearing that you sustained during the attack wouldn't heal on its own, so we needed to stitch your vaginal area and sew your rectum closed in a way to make the healing process a little easier. You will be very sore and will need to take it easy, but after a couple weeks, the pain should go away."

Hearing her say that, I cried. I cried hard.

"There is one last thing, Ms. Neal..." Em started to say.

"Whatever you're about to tell me can't be any worse than anything you've already told me," I said, looking back over at her.

"When you came in, we weren't able to tell at the time because there was a lot of blood, but after running some tests, I saw that you had slightly elevated HCG levels. Performing an ultrasound on you while you were in a coma, my suspicions were confirmed that you were indeed pregnant at the time of the attack, but I'm afraid you lost the baby.

There was so much blood and suctioning going on, when we cleaned you, we must've missed the amniotic sac. The embryo would have already stopped sticking to your uterine wall by this time. I wish I knew more, but I'm sorry, I don't."

"Pregnant? How far along was she?" O'Hajee asked, speaking up for the first time.

"The levels were still low, so I estimate that she was no more than three, maybe four weeks along, but with no embryo, it's hard to determine off the lab work alone," she explained.

Hearing her say that I was pregnant caused my heart to drop. I wasn't sure if I wanted a baby, but the fact that I didn't get to determine that for myself caused my heart to ache. Since the attack happened only a week ago, I knew the baby was O'Hajee's. Looking over at him again, I could see his eyes glistening, but he refused to let the tears fall. His once sad face was now balled up in anger.

"We will let you get some rest since it is a little after five in the morning, but later today, there will be some officers stopping by to take your statement of what happened to you. I know you said you don't remember who they were, but the smallest detail could help them in finding your attackers. When they come, so will your caseworker."

"Caseworker? Why do I need a caseworker?" I questioned confused.

"You're only seventeen, Ms. Neal. We have to report attacks on a child to Child Protective Services."

"I'll be eighteen in like four months."

"I understand that, Ms. Neal, but in the eyes of the law, you are still a child," she explained.

"Look, no disrespect, Dr. James, but I haven't been a child in a very long time. I've been taking care of myself for as long as I can remember, and I don't need no grown ass woman babysitting me. I can take care of my damn self," I snapped.

It wasn't her fault, and I knew she was only doing her job, but they didn't help me when I needed them most. Where the fuck were they seven years ago when my life went to shit? Nowhere to be fucking found, so I damn sure didn't need them now that I was about to be an adult and legally able to live on my own.

"I understand that, and I am sorry, but this cannot be helped. Try to get some rest and I will see you in a couple of hours."

Without saying anything, I nodded my head slowly, and she walked out of the room with the nurse following close behind her.

O'Hajee came over to the bed and looked at the side of my face, but I couldn't look at him if I wanted to. I didn't want to. I needed him, but I didn't want him here.

"Baby," Hajee called out to me, but I put my hand up to stop him.

"I want to see," I told him, not bothering to look up at him.

"C'mon, Z. I'on think you need to see this shit."

"I want to see, Hajee." I repeated.

"Zoie—"

"EITHER HELP ME OR GET THE FUCK OUT, O'HAJEE!" I

snapped, looking in his direction.

Nodding his head slowly, he carefully lifted me into his arms and led me into the bathroom as I pulled the IV stand with us. As he stood me carefully on my feet, I winced a little at the pain I was feeling and stood in front of the full-length mirror with my eyes closed.

Not saying anything, I felt him untie my hospital gown and let it fall off my shoulders. He had to pull it to one side because my IV was in the way, but I no longer felt the fabric on my body, just on my arm.

Opening my eyes slowly, my heart broke in my chest as I looked at all the opened gashes, bruises, and cuts all over my body. There were faint handprints on my wrists and ankles. I cried so hard as I looked at my face. The swelling had gone down, but I had a black eye, and there was bruising along my jawline.

Breaking down in his arms, I slid down to the bathroom floor, and the cold tile soothed the burning I was feeling between my legs.

"C'mon, ma. You can't stay down there. You're going to pop a stitch or somethin'," O'Hajee told me, and without even looking at him, I could hear the tears and pain in his voice.

"Get out," I whispered.

"Ma, you trippin'. I ain't goin' nowhere."

"GET OUT! I FUCKIN' HATE YOU! GET THE FUCK OUT OF MY ROOM!" I screamed.

"You don't mean that."

"Yes the fuck I do! I hate the day I bumped into your stupid ass! Get the fuck away from me, O'Hajee."

"Zoie, please," he pleaded. "I need you, ma. Don't do this."

"You need me?" I scoffed. "Where the fuck was you when I needed you? While I lay in my house, in my bed, and got raped repeatedly. While I got beat and pissed on! Where the fuck was you! Oh, that's right, you were home fucking the bitch that you told me that you didn't want!

Get the fuck away from me, O'Hajee, or I swear to God that I'm going to say fuck being hurt and make sure they give you a room down the hall!" I seethed.

"Baby, I'm sorry. Please don't do this shit."

"Sorry doesn't bring my baby back, O'Hajee. Our baby! Sorry doesn't stop the hate I have for you. Now leave."

"You don't hate me, Zo."

"Yes I do," I growled. "Get the fuck outta my room."

He started to protest, but I held my hand up to stop him.

"Please, O'Hajee. Just go," I said barely above a whisper.

Feeling defeated, he walked out of the bathroom without another word, and a few seconds later, I heard the room door close, and I broke down on the bathroom floor. I couldn't catch a break to save my life, and now I had nothing and no one. This shit couldn't be life.

CHAPTER THREE

Myeke

"*D*oc, how long before he wakes up?" I heard Al ask.

"It's up to him at this point. I can't be too sure," I heard a woman respond.

Seconds later, I heard a door close, and I tried to open my eyes, but no matter how I much I struggled, I couldn't. I felt like my body was a brick of lead. No matter how much I fought against myself, nothing was happening.

Yo, what the fuck is wrong wit' me!

"Have you talked to Hajee?" Al asked.

"Yeah. He was up here yesterday. Zoie woke up and spazzed out on him. From what he said, she lost their baby after her attack. Between both of them being here, he's spiraling. He needs Myeke," my mom explained.

Zoie? Why the fuck is she here? I asked, but no one responded to me.

"Key not gon' want to hear anything he got to say, Ms. Tina. Especially since the same niggas he was fuckin' wit' is the same reason my boy layin' in a hospital bed wit' a tube down his damn throat," Al griped before I heard a popping noise.

I didn't have to have my eyes open to know that my mom had popped him across the back of his head for cussing in front of her. She didn't play that shit at all. She didn't give a damn who you were; she didn't play about disrespect.

But hearing him say that I was in a hospital bed caused me to struggle more against the weight that was on my body. It took all the strength I could muster before I could feel my toes, and I began wiggling them repeatedly before the feeling in my hands started to come back.

"What I say about that damn cussin', Alphonse?"

"Sorry, Mama Tina. You know what I'm sayin' is true. I love Hajee like a little brother, but Key a hot head. He not gon' listen to him. He gon' shoot first and then give him a chance to explain."

"He won't have a choice. I already lost one son, almost lost another one, and I'll be damned if I lose the third over some bullshit that can be handled between them. I may be older, but I'll still beat both of their asses. Fuck I look like," my mom griped.

"Wait, how come you get to cuss but you hit me every time I do it?" Al asked, rewarding him another pop.

"Don't question me, boy. I'm grown!" my mom replied, hitting him again for good measure.

By this time, I had got my eyes to open, and the bright light caused me to wince in pain before I moved my hands and tried to pull at whatever was preventing me from talking.

"Errrrrr," I groaned, trying to sit up.

"Key? Can you hear me, my nigga?" Al asked, rushing over to me.

Nodding my head up and down, I tried to grab the thing in my mouth again, but he stopped me and helped me sit up instead.

"Nah, you can't touch that. Let me call the doctor so they can get you fixed up."

Nodding my head, I looked in the direction of my mom, and she had tears in her eyes and her hand over her mouth.

"Thank God!" she cried before rushing over to me and falling into my chest.

I winced a little from the pain that shot through me. Leaning up with an apologetic look on her face, she backed up and stood next to me, rubbing my head.

"I'm sorry, baby. I'm just happy that you're up," she told me, smiling. "You've been out so long, I didn't think you would ever wake up."

Confused, I raised an eyebrow and waited for her to explain, but before she could, Al came back in the room with a doctor.

"Look at God; your family is two for two this week. First Ms. Neal, and now you, Mr. Compton," she said with a smile on her face, going to the sink and washing her hands. "My name is Emily James, but you can call me Em. I know you have a lot of questions, but let me get this tube out of your throat first before we go any further, okay?" she asked.

Nodding my head slightly, I watched as she slid on gloves and began to unstrap the tub that was in my mouth. I watched her intently, and I had to admit to myself that Dr. James was bad as fuck. She couldn't have been much older than me, and the color of her smooth chestnut skin had me wanting to reach out and lick her.

Sticking some little tube down my throat, she sprayed something down my throat before she started to pull on the bigger tube that was in my throat, causing me to growl at the pain.

"I'm sorry. I know it's uncomfortable. I'm trying to be gentle." She apologized as she pulled at the tube a little more until it was completely out. "Now, don't try to talk just yet. Let me get you some water."

Never taking my eyes off her, I nodded my head and watched her walk to the water pitcher and pour me a cup, before walking back over to me and placing the cup at my lips.

Taking the first sip soothed my burning throat, and I drank the water so fast that I started to choke and go into a coughing fit.

"Easy, Mr. Compton," she chided. "Easy."

"Key," I told her in a raspy voice.

"Excuse me?" she asked, confused.

"Call me Key."

Smiling slightly, she nodded her head before taking the cup away from my lips and placing it on the little bed table beside us. I guess my staring was making her uncomfortable because she broke eye contact with me before putting a little distance between us.

Finally stopping my eye assault, I looked over at where Al and my mom stood. My mom had a raised eyebrow, and Al wore a smirk. I guess they saw me eye fucking the doctor too, but I ain't care. Shorty was bad as hell.

"Now, your throat will be a little sore but, for the most part, you should be fine. Just take it easy, okay?"

"Yes, ma'am," I replied, giving her a lopsided smile.

"Good. Now, Mr. Compton—" she started until she saw the look on my face. "I mean Key. You were dropped off at our emergency entrance, about a week ago, covered in blood. You were shot a total of eleven times. Most of the bullets missed a vital organ and went in and out, minus the one that ruptured your spleen.

Due to the damage, we had to remove it. Without a spleen, you can live a very full life, except you have to be a little more cautious of the things you're around and what you eat. Without it, you're more susceptible to infections, but you will be alive and well, nonetheless," she explained.

"Damn, eleven? That's a lot of bullets," I said, shaking my head.

"Yeah, my nigga. Now ya ass can outdo 50 Cent's ass. Everyone be bragging about him being shot nine times and living to tell about it," Al joked.

Shaking her head, my mom popped his ass again, causing him to flinch, and I laughed a little. It was one thing to hear my mom hit him, but to actually see his big ass wince was something totally different in itself.

"That shit isn't funny, Alphonse," my mom chided.

"Yes, ma'am."

Shaking her head, a smile danced on the doctor's lips, and it had me wondering what she looked like in a full-blown smile. Her lips were sexy as hell, and I got a small glimpse of her white teeth, but I was curious. I wanted to see the full thing, and I wanted to be the cause of that smile.

"As I was saying, you are going to have to undergo months of physical therapy, but I am confident that within three months or so, you should be able to walk without a limp, and you should be running in six."

"Will I be doing therapy with you?" I asked.

"No. I'm afraid I'm not a physical therapist. Just a plain ol' surgeon," she explained, shaking her head.

"I'on think nothin' is plain about being a surgeon, ma. Especially not where I'm from."

"Well, thank you. I think."

"No problem. Now when can I get outta here?"

"Oh no, Mr. Compton. You aren't going anywhere. You will be here for at least another three weeks."

"Bro, I can't fuckin' stay here for three weeks. I got shit to do, and laying up in a hospital ain't one of them," I told her, kissing my teeth.

"Well, I don't know what to tell you, Mr. Compton—"

"Key." I corrected her.

"Excuse me, Key. Though there is nothing I can do if you choose to check yourself out of this hospital in another three days or so, it will be against my medical opinion for you to leave.

You've had too much damage done, and you can not only pop one of your stitches, but you can also get an infection in your blood, and that will kill you if you're not here. You can barely walk and get around on your own. Leaving would be a very bad idea. You just underwent four surgeries and, not to mention, almost lost your life. It would be stupid to leave," she snapped, and I had to raise an eyebrow at her.

"If I didn't know any better, Doc, I'd swear you cared," I told her.

"I care about all my patients," she replied.

"Yeah, aight. Well, I'on know what to tell you, shorty, but I'm—"

"Goin' to stay your high yellow ass in that damn bed until they say it's okay for you to leave here." My mom interrupted what I was about to say.

"But, Ma."

"Shut the hell up talking to me, Myeke, or I'm going to forget that your lil' ass is in a hospital bed and come over there and fuck you up," Moms snapped at me, and I ain't even going to front; a nigga folded his arms over his chest and pouted like a little ass kid.

I hated fucking hospitals, and I wasn't trying to be a fucking pin cushion while they tried to nurse a nigga back to health. All I needed was some weed, a lil' alcohol, and some pain meds, and a nigga would be good. Back to business as usual.

"Don't worry, Dr. James; he isn't goin' anywhere, and if he tries, I will trip his overgrown ass," my mom told Emily, and that caused her to break out into a full smile.

"Well, I guess that means that I won't have any problems out of you then, Key, huh?" Emily asked turning around to look at me.

"Oh, nah, shorty, that ain't what that means at all. I'ma still talk shit, but as long as you my doctor, I guess a nigga can try to be on his best behavior," I told her with a wink.

"I guess that's better than nothing."

"Oh definitely." I smiled. "Now, I'on know if I heard you right before, but lil' sis is here too?" I asked.

"You must mean Ms. Neal."

"Yeah."

"Well, I'm not allowed to discuss a patient's condition with anyone, but your brother assured me that you were family when I spoke with him the night you two were brought in.

Ms. Neal was brutally raped and beaten a little over a week ago. O'Hajee brought her in because she had gone into shock, and her heart was failing. I was able to revive her, but she lost the baby," she explained.

"Baby? Wait, she was pregnant?" Moms asked, walking over to her.

"According to her blood levels, she couldn't have been any further along than a few weeks. Too early for her to have known. I informed her and Mr. Compton of the news yesterday when she woke up."

"Damn, lil' sis can't catch a break. Can I see her?"

"Maybe tomorrow, if you're both up to it. For now, I want to try and get some food in your system and monitor you closely."

"Whatever you say, Doc."

"Good. Now I'll allow you guys to talk. I will be back to check on you a little later."

"Thank you," we all said in unison as she smiled again and walked back out the room.

"Leave her alone, Myeke," my mom spoke as soon as the door closed.

"What you talkin' about? I ain't did nothing," I responded with a goofy smile on my face.

"I can see it all in your face. You already got one MIA female, and you can't afford to add another to the list when you have a family at home. Speaking of which, where the hell is Siya and my grandson?"

Just the mention of Siya's name shifted my whole mood, and the smile fell from my face. Remembering that she was the reason I was in this hospital bed, I grimaced as thoughts of murder ran rapid through my mind.

"I ain't worried about that bitch! If it wasn't for her, I wouldn't be layin' here. My only concern is hunting her ass down so that I can find my son and then after that, that hoe can play in traffic for all I care." I seethed.

"What you mean, she the reason you here?" Al asked, and I shook my head.

I wasn't about to have this conversation in front of my mom. I had already said too much, and I couldn't put that burden on her of knowing that Siya was the one that set me up to get wet up. I'd deal with Siya in my own way; for now, I needed to handle the snake that I called my little brother.

"Another time, my nigga. For now, I need to get in touch wit' the lil' nigga that my moms gave birth to."

"First of all, you will not disrespect him in front of me. As far as O'Hajee goes, I will go get him for you to hear what he has to say,

39

Myeke, but the moment that you threaten him or put your hands on him, I will smack fire from your ass my damn self. Do you understand me?"

Rolling my eyes in my head, I smacked my lips and just looked at her. I wasn't agreeing to that shit because, depending on what he said, I may drop that little nigga where he stood.

"I ain't agreeing to that shit," I finally said.

"Either you agree to it or you won't see him, and ya ass will be left in the dark."

"No disrespect, but you must've forgot who I am. With or without you bringing him to me, it's only so far he can hide before I touch him. The only reason he has ever been untouchable is off the strength that the lil' nigga got my blood running through his veins."

I watched as my mom's eyes went into slits, and she walked over to me with the nastiest grimace on her face, before closing the distance and leaning forward. Grabbing a handful of my hair, she snatched my head back and her voice got low.

"And you must forget that it's my fuckin' blood that runs through yours. You starting to smell yourself because this ain't what the fuck you want. You must've forgot who the fuck I am!" she snapped. "But let me fuckin' remind you; I was the one that showed you how to bust a gun. Ya daddy may have taught you what he knew about the dope game, but I was the one that made sure you could cook that shit.

I was the one in the field with you. Am I proud of that shit? No. But you forget that I can body you in this fucking hospital bed and walk away like shit didn't happen. Now, like I said, when I go get my son, you will not touch him, or I touch you. Do you fuckin' understand me?" she growled, pulling my hair tighter.

Staring back into my mom's cold eyes, I had to admit that I had let the shit slip out my memory that my moms was a fucking savage before she got on drugs. She taught me a lot of what I know. Shit, me and Rod. She was a Brooklyn chick for real, and she reminded me why she had bitches and niggas shook back in her prime.

"Yeah, I hear you," I replied as she let my hair go.

"Good. Now I'll be back," she said, her eyes returning to normal and giving me a kiss on my forehead, before she walked out the room like she didn't just threaten my life.

"Bro, I dead ass forgot that Ms. Tina was a fuckin' goon back in the day." Al fell out laughing when she left the room.

"Shit, me too, my nigga," I replied, rubbing the sore spot in my head.

"She had you lookin' like a bitch the way she was pulling your hair. I was waiting for her ass to pull out a strap, my nigga. Dead ass. You had moms tight as fuck." He laughed, and I grilled his ass because I ain't see shit funny. "But on the real, I think you should hear what Haj got to say," he said once he stopped laughing.

"And why should I do that?"

"One, he ya lil' brother, and I got mad love for the lil' nigga, and two, I couldn't see him snaking you. He loves you too much for that shit."

Instead of responding, I just nodded my head and started trying to mentally prepare myself for what was about to come. I didn't want to write my lil' brother off, but I'd go in that nigga's shit if he said something to me I didn't like. I'd just have to deal with moms later.

God, please give me strength. I'on wanna kill my lil' brother, but I will, I thought, laying my head back and staring at a spot on the ceiling. Yeah, something had to give, and this was the first piece to the puzzle I needed. I just hoped God heard my prayer.

CHAPTER FOUR

O'Hajee

*M*y mom calling me and telling me that Myeke was awake, had me relieved and terrified at the same time. For the past week, I tried to come up with a way to explain this situation to him without him beating my ass, but I didn't see one.

No matter how I looked at it, I was wrong, and I had to deal with the consequences of my actions like a grown ass man. I made my own bed, so now it was time that I lay in it. Taking a deep breath, I said a quick prayer and asked God to look over me before placing my sweaty palms on the room door and pushing it open.

My eyebrows dipped in confusion when I didn't see him lying in the bed, but then I heard the toilet flush before the door swung open and he hobbled out. I could tell each step he took was taking a lot out of him, so I reached out to help him, and he swatted my hand out the way before grimacing at me.

"All I'm tryin' to do is help," I offered.

"Just like you helped them niggas rob my spot, and took my

money and my dope?" he shot back, and I was confused as hell.

"Bro, why the fuck would I steal from you? That shit don't even make sense."

"First off, nigga, I ain't ya fuckin' brother. But since you so innocent, explain to me why I found the shit in the bottom of your closet in your backpack. Shit had to be yours, right?" he questioned.

"Of course it was mine, but it's not what you think it is. I didn't know that was your dope."

"Then why the fuck did you have it?"

"That's what I been tryin' to tell you," I said, rubbing my hand down my face. I was trying to find the easiest way to admit what I had done, but I couldn't find the words.

"If I wasn't confined to this hospital bed, I'd go in ya mouth, my nigga. Dead ass. I knew you had ya ways about you, but I never pegged you for a grimy ass nigga. Just a fuckin' goof. Al, can you believe this nigga?" he asked Al, letting off a pissed off chuckle as if he didn't just insult me to my face.

"You fuckin' buggin', B. I understand you tight right now, but I ain't about to let you keep disrespecting me like I ain't put my fuckin' life on the line for ya ass. Brother or not, I swear I'm this close to sayin' fuck ya forgiveness."

"You said that shit to say what, my nigga? Do you know how many times I done had to put my life on the line for ya bitch ass? Do you know who was out in the streets making sure you had a roof over ya head, while moms was out getting high?"

"My nigga, don't try to get all high and mighty now; we live in the motherfuckin' projects, B. Rent ain't that fuckin' high," I snapped.

I was trying to compose myself, but this nigga was really on one, and I had to remind myself that this shit was my fault, and I needed to get my anger in check, but I was this close to opening back up one of his stitches.

"But the shit ain't free, my nigga! You so busy running around this bitch wantin' to play motherfuckin' king of Brooklyn, but you ain't never had to put that fuckin' work in, my nigga. I did! I was the fuckin' one out there, nickel and diming so that ya ass didn't have to take my fuckin' hand me downs.

I was the one making sure ya ungrateful ass was good! Who the fuck dropped out of school to take care of ya ignorant ass? Nobody but fuckin' me. So don't sit here and say you ever did somethin' for me, when ya selfish ass don't give a fuck about no one but ya damn self!" he barked.

"Nigga, suck my dick. I should've let that nigga body ya ass!" I snapped back.

"What the fuck you say to me, my nigga?" he asked, his eyes closed into slits, and if he was a cartoon character, his light-skinned ass would have smoke coming out of his fucking ear.

"You heard what the fuck I said, son, or you wouldn't have asked me to repeat it. But since you think a nigga selfish, let my selfish ass enlighten you. I tried to warn your hard-headed ass not to come out the fuckin' house the night that you got shot after I bodied that nigga Sac. I tried to warn you, but you were so hell bent on coming to make me pay; yet, if you had just fuckin' listened for once in your life, we wouldn't be where the fuck we are!

You right, a nigga fucked up by dealing wit' Deuce behind ya back, but not once in my life have I ever let that nigga disrespect you, and we've had words plenty of times about you. The shit may look like some snake shit on your end up, but nothin' about what I was doing was because I fuckin' hated you or liked that nigga. It was about earnin' shit on my own! You don't think I knew the shit that you did for me when moms was out gettin' high before you threw that bullshit in my fuckin' face! Ain't no respect in a grown ass man that can't make a way on their own.

I've never in my life had to use the gun Rod gave me until last week, and I split a nigga's shit wide open because I overheard him talking about bodying you wit' that nigga Deuce, and I've been lookin' for his hoe ass since, but since I can't find him and I'm such a fuckin' snake ass nigga, I'll let you handle your shit. If you don't forgive me, then fuck it, my nigga. Between the fuckin' nightmares and feelin' sorry for myself, I can check your bullshit off the damn list. Fuck outta here!" I seethed.

I watched with fury in my eyes as his face softened at the news that I had killed Sac for him, but fuck Myeke. If that nigga wanted to be mad at me for trying to stand on my own two feet, then oh fucking well. I was dead ass wrong for dealing with Deuce on that level, but hindsight was 20/20, and I couldn't take the shit back now. All I could do was live with my consequences.

"Haj," he started to say, rubbing his hand down his face, but I shook my head.

"Save it, bro. Do ya thing, and I'ma hunt down the niggas that violated my girl. I accept the fact that the only brother I had is dead," I told him and turned around to walk out the room.

"Hajee," Al started.

"We good, my nigga," I told him before walking out the room.

When the door closed behind me, I tightly closed my eyes, and the lone tear that I had been holding rolled down my cheek, before I walked off. I loved my brother to death, but I wasn't about to beg that nigga for shit. If he still felt the way he felt after everything I said, then nothing I ever said would change his feelings. For now, I was pushing this shit to the back of my mind. I had bigger shit to worry about, and her name was Zoie Neal.

CHAPTER FIVE

Zoie

The next day

$\mathcal{I}$ couldn't sleep for anything in the world after I kicked O'Hajee out of my room, and he had been sending me messages ever since. I guess he must've found a way to get me some clothes, my phone, and wallet from my apartment when I was in the coma, and I was grateful that he did because nothing could make me go back in that apartment after what happened.

I had nightmares all night and had woken up around three a.m., and I'd been up since. I heard a knock on the room door and looked over at the clock that read ten-fifteen. The nurse had just come from doing my vitals around nine, so I knew she wasn't back already.

"Come in," I called out and pulled myself up in the bed as best I could.

It was uncomfortable as hell sitting down, but my arm kept falling asleep, and I wasn't trying to have bed sores from laying in one position

49

for too long. I kept my eyes trained on the door as it was pushed open some, and Dr. James came in pushing Myeke in a wheelchair.

My heart instantly dropped to my stomach, and I tried to get out the bed but winced from the pain that shot through my lower abdomen.

"Yo, sis, sit ya ass down somewhere," Myeke said with a slight grin on his face.

"Oh my gosh, Key. What happened to you?" I gasped.

"I hope it's okay that I brought him up here, Zoie. He has been asking to see you since he woke up last night," Em spoke up before he had a chance to answer my question.

"Yes, it's fine."

"Great. Well, I'm going to leave you two alone, and I'll be back in about thirty minutes to take you down to get checked out by the physical therapist, Mr. Compton," she said, causing Myeke to shoot her a look over his shoulder.

Rolling her eyes playfully in her head, she looked at him, and he stared back at her like he was waiting for something.

"Key." She corrected herself with a small smile on her face.

Giving her a cocky smirk, he looked back over at me and winked at me, while she stood there like I caught her doing something that she wasn't supposed to be doing.

"I'll leave you two to it," she said, leaving the room, not waiting on a reply.

"What was that about?" I asked when she closed the door behind her.

"What was what?" he asked, feigning ignorance.

"Bro, don't play. I see you over there flirting with the doctor."

"Who, Em? That's nothing."

"And we're on a first name basis, *Key*," I joked, putting emphasis on his name.

"You buggin'." He laughed. "But on the real, I kind of heard about what happened from Hajee yesterday. How you feelin'?"

Shrugging my shoulders, I didn't really want to think about it, but the way he was looking at me, I could tell I wasn't going to get away without giving him something.

"I guess I'm fine. I'm sore, and I've been having some chest pains, but I'm alive, right?"

"That don't mean shit tho', ma. Don't get me wrong; a nigga happy as hell to see you still standing, but that don't mean shit if you shutting down and not dealin' wit' the shit," he told me.

"I am dealin' with it."

"And how you doin' that?"

When I got quiet, he gave me a knowing look, and I just dropped my head. I wasn't in the right state of mind to talk about this shit.

"Have you told Hajee exactly what happened?" he asked, changing the line of questioning when he saw I wasn't able to answer the previous one.

"With all due respect, fuck your brother," I spat, rolling my eyes up in my head.

Chuckling, he shook his head and ran his hand down his face.

51

"He on your shit list too, huh?" he asked.

"I walked in on him fuckin' her," I whispered.

"Fuckin' who?"

"Monica."

"Damn," was all he could say.

I couldn't really blame him though, because I didn't know what to say either.

"I may be pissed at the lil' nigga right now, but I'd never kick the nigga's back in. He loves you, Zoie. The nigga in a fucked-up headspace right now, but he do," he told me, and I looked up at him again.

Instead of replying, I just nodded my head and thought about what he said. I didn't doubt for once that O'Hajee loved me, but I had enough shit on my mind than to have to deal with our broken relationship.

"Enough about me tho'. What happened?" I asked, pointing at the wheelchair.

"Can you believe them niggas tried to Pac me?" he joked. "Shot my shit up, but you know it's hard to kill real nigga." He smirked.

"What happened?"

"It ain't important."

"Does it have anything to do with why you aren't speaking with O'Hajee?" I asked, even though I was pretty sure that I knew the answer.

"At first I thought it did, but now I'on know what to believe. I love the lil' nigga to death, but that doesn't change the fact that the nigga snaked me," he replied, and I already knew what he was referring to.

"I told him he should've told you," I said, shaking my head.

"Told me what?"

"About the guy. He was scared though."

"Of?"

"For you to hate him. He told me that you didn't listen to shit; that once you came up with an answer in your mind, nothing could ever stray you from it until you felt the need to change it. Like, you're too stubborn to see past anything else," I told him.

Running his hand through his bushy hair, he sat back and just looked at me. From his demeanor, I could tell that what O'Hajee said about him was true. And if I knew O'Hajee the way that I believed I did, he would tell the truth, but he wouldn't beg Myeke. He was one of those people that would tell you the truth, but he would let you believe what you wanted. His thing was, why convince someone of something that they feel they already know. In a way, it made sense, but I didn't think he should look at this situation that way.

"I think you should hear him out though," I told him, breaking the silence.

"I will, if you will."

"I'm not ready for that, and I don't think I will be any time soon," I admitted.

"It may not seem like it now, sis, but you still got us. We ain't went nowhere; regardless of what y'all going through, me and moms got you. Now, I'on know how much use a nigga can be to you in this fuckin' wheelchair, but if a nigga come close, I'm fuckin' that nigga ankles up, B," he said, and I fell out laughing.

I could tell that he was serious as hell too, and I could imagine this nigga rolling over people's toes in a wheelchair, but I was glad that he was okay. We talked a little more, and he told me that if I needed anything from him just to call Ms. Tina, and she would get Al. When the doctor came back in and got him, he promised to come back and see me every day, and I was happy because I could use the company.

* * *

Waking up to a light flashing in my face, I stirred in the bed and almost pissed on myself as a man stood over me with a camera. Jumping up, I pulled the thin sheet back over my body and looked around the room.

There was a total of five people in the room, standing around, and Emily was one of them. She apologized to me with her eyes but kept speaking with the police officer that was scribbling something down in his notebook.

"Yo, what the fuck? You couldn't wake me up before you started takin' pictures of me? That shit is corny as hell!" I snapped.

I wasn't trying to come off as rude, but the mean mug on my face didn't seem to move the guy with the camera one bit as he took picture after picture. When he tried to reach to tilt my head to the side, I smacked his hand away from me so fast that he almost lost balance.

"Ms. Neal, I apologize if we startled you, but I need pictures of the damage done to your face for my case files. My name is Shelia Bradford. I'm a caseworker at child services, and I've been assigned your case," the woman in the suit spoke up, and I gave her the once over, never accepting the hand she had extended toward me.

When she realized that I wasn't going to shake her hand or say anything, she continued.

"We've been trying to get in touch with your mother," she said, looking down at the folder she had in her hands. "Brenda Neal. Do you know where we can find her?"

"Do you think I can? She isn't here apparently, so she obviously isn't too worried about me and, trust, the feeling is mutual," I replied.

"Zoie, I understand that you are upset, but—"

"*Upset?*" I repeated, cutting her off. "You are *upset* when you stump your toe. You are *upset* when you spill a cup of juice on your favorite shirt. What I am right now is everything but fucking *upset.*" I snarled.

Could you believe this bitch? What she failed to realize was I knew that my mom's crackhead ass wasn't going to be here, especially when she had a hand in why I was in this bed. I learned a long time ago that she didn't give a damn about me, and she never would. In the beginning, it hurt because I didn't know who my father was, and I never got the love I wanted from my mother.

It hardened me, but I survived all the other bullshit, so I was sure I would survive this too—by myself like I always did. She was in the right ballpark when she said I was upset, but that wasn't the right word to use. I felt like ol' girl on *Diary of a Mad Black Woman*. I was mad as hell!

"Maybe we should do this some other time," Emily suggested, speaking up for the first time. "Zoie has gone through a lot, and her heart is already recovering from the attack, as well as her body, and we don't want to upset her or cause her any kind of stress that could send her backwards."

"I understand your concern, Dr. James, but Zoie will have to deal with this one way or another. It's already been made clear that she doesn't remember what happened, from what you told me, but that doesn't change the fact that when she leaves here that she will not be going home. She will be sent to a group home."

"Group home? It's not like I'm a little kid. I will be eighteen in a few months. I don't need a group home. I need to be left alone!"

"Zoie, they're just trying to help," Emily said, rubbing my shoulder.

"You're about seven years too late for that. When I needed your help, you guys were nowhere around. When I was going to the hospital for cigarette burns, broken arms, and fractured ribs, where the fuck were you then!

Oh, don't look so surprised. You forget, I grew up in the gutter, lady. You've seen the reports, and I know you've read my case file to know that this isn't my first walk in the park. Caseworkers been running in and out of my house since I could talk, and no one ever felt the need to *help* me then. Brenda would clean up for a few days, pass an inspection, and you guys would disappear, saying you didn't have enough evidence to proceed.

You believed that bitch when she said I was doing all that shit to myself. What seven-year-old do you know will sit there and willingly burn themselves over sixteen times, with a lit cigarette, on their stomach? So, you can save all your fake ass concern. I understand you got a job to do, but I'm not it. All the damage is already done on my end. You and this fucked up system could have prevented this, but you didn't, and I don't need you now. Like I said, I'll be eighteen soon, but if I need to get emancipated before then, believe me, I will. But I refuse to go to your fucked-up ass group home. Bitch, you'll have to arrest me first!"

By the time I finished speaking, Emily had tears in her eyes, and everyone's mouths in the room were hitting the floor. I wasn't shocked though, because they knew they'd fucked up, and if I wanted to take this shit further and sue the state for dropping the ball, then I could, but I didn't feel it was necessary.

Before I looked over, I smelled his cologne. He must've slipped in when I was reading this uppity bitch like a book, but I refused to look at him. I was happy he was here but, at the same time, I didn't want to be anywhere near him.

"Now, unless you want a lawsuit coming, I'd suggest that you leave me alone. Oh, and don't worry, there are plenty of lawyers that would love to prosecute the State of New York. All it takes is one phone call and a happy DA to take you down, and I'm sure they don't want that on their hands," I threatened.

I had no intentions on calling a lawyer, but this bitch didn't need to know that. They wouldn't be getting a check off me, and if they tried, my ass would just run away. This was fucking Brooklyn; they wouldn't be coming to look for me no time soon, if at all.

"Maybe we should continue this another time," the caseworker said, straightening out her suit. "Good day, Ms. Neal. Dr. James," she added before stepping out of the room, with everyone that she brought with her walking out close behind her.

"Good riddance," I mumbled, falling back on the bed, closing my eyes.

"Zoie, I think you could have handled that a lot better. They still have a job to do," Emily explained.

"And it looks like I do too, Doc. No disrespect, but I been doing this long enough on my own; they don't want anything but a paycheck, and I won't be the source of them getting it. When I get out of here, I will go through the process of getting emancipated. Rather it be four months or four years, I can't get lost in the system," I explained.

"But how are you going to pay for a lawyer?"

"I got her," O'Hajee spoke up finally, stepping further in the room. "She good regardless," he told her.

"Mr. Compton, nice to see you again."

"Call me Haj or Hajee," he told her.

"You and your brother both must hate your real names, huh?" she asked him with a smirk on her face.

"Key does. Only two people call me O'Hajee, and no one calls me Mr. Compton, shorty. I'm too young for that." He laughed. "I know you gotta be professional and shit, but Hajee is fine when you're in here with us."

"I'll have to remember that, Hajee," she told him before turning back to me. "If you need anything when you get out of here, don't hesitate to ask. I'm going to get the nurse to bring you lunch, and then I will take you down to the lab to get some x-rays done and a cat scan. If everything checks out, you can be leaving as early as tomorrow night."

"Thanks, Em," I told her with a weak smile.

"You're welcome. I'll be back. Don't stress her out, Hajee. Please, or she'll be in here a lot longer than expected."

"Too late," I mumbled as she walked out of the room.

Silence fell over the room, and I could feel his eyes on the side of my face, but I refused to look at him. I wasn't ready to talk to him, but I knew I couldn't avoid him forever.

"You just gon' ignore me, mama?" he asked, taking a seat on the foot of the hospital bed.

Instead of responding, I looked over at him with an emotionless expression on my face. Even though my face held no emotion, my heart was racing in my chest, and my clit made that familiar thumping that I had gotten accustomed to whenever he was around.

I was happy as hell that the nurse let me take off the heart monitor probes, or this room would be going crazy with that loud ass beeping. Looking him over, he looked like shit. He had bags under his eyes, he needed a line up, and his eyes were bloodshot red, but he was still sexy as hell. The sadness behind his eyes had me wanting to reach out to hold him and tell him that everything would be okay, but I couldn't tell him that, because I didn't know if it was true myself.

"What do you want, O'Hajee?" I asked in a flat tone.

"You."

"You had me, remember, and you pushed me away, and I still

59

don't know why, but that doesn't change the fact that not only did you abandon me without so much as a word, but you were fucking that bitch Monica in the bed that you held me in every other night."

"I fucked up, baby," he said, running his hand down his face.

"That's all you can say? You fucked up?" I asked with a raised eyebrow.

"What you want me to say, Zoie? I fucked up, ma, and I'll do whatever I gotta do to fix it," he said, scooting toward me and placing his hand on my thigh.

"Don't touch me," I hissed. "Just tell me why? What did I do?"

"Nah, ma, this shit wasn't you. It was me. I can't explain it; I wish I could, but I can't," he stated in a stressed tone.

"What the hell you mean, you can't, O'Hajee?"

"I just can't, ma. Just tell me how to fix it."

"Can you un-fuck Monica? Can you take back the times that you ignored my calls, my text messages? Can you give me my virginity back?" I questioned.

"C'mon, ma. You know I can't do that."

"Then we have nothing to talk about," I responded.

"That's not fair. You can't just walk away, ma. I know I fucked up, but I need you," he told me, sadness dripping from his voice.

"What the fuck is up with everyone that is in the wrong, telling me what I can't do? Get the fuck outta here. You gotta be stupid as hell."

"Zoie. Please," he whispered.

Closing my eyes tight, the pain in his voice almost made me crack a little, but I couldn't give in. I loved O'Hajee with everything in me, but I wouldn't be his plaything. Who was to say that when we got back on track, he wouldn't pull the same stunt and go out and fuck bitches again? I knew he cared about me, but I wasn't that damn naïve. Niggas crawled their way back when they knew they fucked up, but the moment you let your guard down, more bullshit followed.

"I think it's time for you to leave," I whispered, opening my eyes back.

Nodding his head up and down slowly, he stood to his feet and started to walk toward the door again. I closed my eyes and waited for him to leave, but he walked back over towards me and grabbed my chin in his hands gently.

"Look at me, ma," he demanded softly.

Waving my head side to side, I kept them closed and fought back the tears that I felt building up. My mouth was telling him to leave, and my mind was telling me that it was the right thing to do, but my heart was screaming for him to come back, and I knew if I looked in his eyes that I would want him to.

"C'mon, ma. Just look at me."

Counting to ten in my mind to get myself together, I took a deep breath before opening my eyes and staring back up into his. His eyes were glossy, and the love they held in them scared me, but the fear in them crushed my soul even more.

"I love you, Zoie Elizabeth Neal, and I swear if it's the last thing I do, I'ma make this shit up to you. Now isn't the right time to tell you what happened, because you don't need that extra stress on your back. But when I tell you that I won't stop until I have ya heart back, I mean that shit from the bottom of my heart.

I will never stop fighting for you, ma. You got a nigga's mind, body, and soul, and I know I got the same. I'ma give you some space, but I'll be back tomorrow to check on you," he told me before leaning down and kissing me with so much intensity that it scared me.

Closing my eyes, I allowed a tear to fall as I returned the kiss, before he pulled back, causing me to open my eyes again. Reaching his thumb up, he wiped away the lone tear before wiping away one of his own and letting go of the loose grip he had on my chin.

Without another word, he walked out the room, and I swear my heart went with him. For the first time, I cried over O'Hajee. I cried for him and what he was going through, and the damage that was done to us. I just prayed that we could get back on track because if we didn't, I wasn't sure how either of us would survive.

CHAPTER SIX

Deuce

"*The number you have called is no longer in service. If you believe that you have reached this message in error, please hang up and try your call again.*"

This was my third time in a row hearing this message, and I still pressed the call button again to get the same exact message. Slamming my phone on the dresser, I took a sip of the brandy that I had in my hand, and welcomed the burn.

I had been calling Siya since last week, and the bitch had turned her phone off. I went by Mom's house, and of course she wasn't there, and because that pretty nigga moved her out of the hood, I didn't know where she stayed at.

"How the fuck is this nigga still alive?" I growled at the workers that were sitting in my living room.

"We don't know, Deuce. That nigga was laying on the ground, soaked in blood when we left. He didn't even look like he was breathing," the younger one named Haywire spoke up.

"Yeah. We unloaded our whole clips in that nigga's truck," Sleeze added.

"If that was the case, I wouldn't be getting a fuckin' call from a jawn at the hospital sayin' that nigga was breathing!" I barked. "Knew I shouldn't have left you incompetent motherfuckas to do anything for me."

"Incompetent? What the fuck does that supposed to mean?" Levi asked with dipped eyebrows.

"You don't know what the fuck incompetent means, dummy?" Hay asked him. "He called us stupid."

"Actually, he called us useless," Sleeze corrected.

Shaking my head, I pinched the bridge of my nose to calm myself down before I shot all three of these dummies in their face.

"Yo! Shut the fuck up, bruh! Like, y'all is fuckin' retarded! You need to figure out how the fuck you gon' fix your fuck up! That nigga breathin', and he gon' know it was us," I snapped.

"He don't even know us. What you expect, us to walk up in that jawn, knocking motherfuckas down?" Levi asked, confused.

I was three seconds away from killing his ass, but these were the only people on my crew I could get in touch with. After they got wind that O'Hajee splattered Sac's brains all over my room, and the hit on Myeke didn't go as planned, they dipped out. I had about twenty niggas on my team before, but now that all of them folded, all I had was me and the three stooges over here.

I was sure that Myeke had gotten wind that I was behind all this shit, but I wasn't sure if he knew Siya's involvement in everything, and she'd better pray to God that, that nigga got to her before I did because I was gon' kill her hoe ass with my bare hands. Sister or not.

After going in my safe, I realized all my dope was gone, and I had about ten racks to my name. I was down bad, and I needed to get back on, but right now, Key's work wasn't an option. The nigga may have been out of commission, but Al was running shit and had changed all the spots around. I didn't have enough people to scope out where they were, and I couldn't get shit on consignment, because my plug told me he wasn't fucking with me at all.

He got wind of what the fuck happened, and he already said that he wasn't fucking with it. Too much heat. If Myeke didn't cause problems in my life, the Feds would be right around the corner waiting, and he didn't need that type of heat. And to be real, neither did I, but I was in it now, so what choice did I have.

Dialing Siya's number again, I got the same recording as the first time, and my anger started to rise again. I didn't know what the fuck I was going to do, but I needed to do the shit fast. I was broke, hiding, and pissed the hell off. All I knew for sure was, I had to get to this nigga Key before he got to me, or shit would only get worse.

CHAPTER SEVEN

Siya

"You don't think you need to put some clothes on?" I heard Mark ask, stepping into the kitchen.

I had a glass of orange juice in my hands, standing with my hair pulled in a messy bun on top of my head. I had on a cropped sweatshirt that showed off my belly button ring, and some shorts that barely covered my butt cheeks. I was lounging around the house, and I was comfortable.

Giving him the once over, I let my eyes stop on the bulge that stuck out in his gray sweatpants, and smirked when it swung as he started walking further into a kitchen. The sweats hung off his waist, and his chiseled chest was bare and dripping sweat like he had been working hard.

"Shouldn't I be asking you the same question?" I finally asked back, setting my cup on the counter.

"Difference is, this is my house. You just visiting," he shot back.

"Not from what Syd says. You have your own place, right, so you don't have to be here."

"Neither do you, but we both are," he replied with a grimace on his face.

Even with as mean as he looked, I smirked at him. Mark was sexy, and his attitude just turned me on even more. If I was a grimy bitch, he could get it, but I was trying to do right. Well, sort of.

"You gon' keep undressing a nigga, or are you gon' go put some clothes on? I know Syd wouldn't appreciate that shit."

Rolling my eyes up in my head, I drank the last bit of my juice and put my cup in the sink.

"Nigga, please. You act like I'm supposed to be afraid of Sydney."

"No, but you should respect her and her space. You a guest, in case you forgot, but pushing up on her nigga and walking around her house half naked like she don't got one, ain't cool," he commented.

"Ain't nobody even checkin' for your ugly ass," I told him, sucking my teeth.

"Who you tryna play, shorty? We both know that if I was trying to fuck you, I could. You probably wet as fuck right now just thinking about me sliding this monster up in that loose ass pussy." He smirked.

Just as the words left his lips, my clit thumped, and my panties got moist. He was right; I could imagine it, but wasn't nothing about this pussy loose, and he'd better leave me the fuck alone before I showed him what the fuck he was missing. Look, I said I was trying but, in the end, I knew I was still a grimy bitch, and I would fuck Mark so good he would be questioning his own masculinity.

"Fuck you, bum ass nigga. Ain't nobody worried about your tired ass. One thing this pussy ain't is loose, and I guarantee that before it's all said and done, it'll be you sweating me, not the other way around," I shot back before turning to walk out of the kitchen.

I didn't have to look back to know that he was watching me leave the kitchen, so in true Siya fashion, I gave his ass something to look at. Yeah, before it was all said and done, I would have to fuck Mark to show him who the fuck was in charge, but I was up for the job. Anything to keep him out of my way.

* * *

"Girl, shit has been crazy. First, them niggas hitting Key, and now the police kickin' in niggas' doors. This shit OD crazy. I just wish I would've known Key's ass was sending you and Karson on vacation. I would've tried to come along, but then again, that means I wouldn't have Hajee back on my team," Monica said.

I rolled my eyes so hard that I swore they almost got stuck. Everyone in the hood knew that O'Hajee didn't want Monica's ass, and if what I was hearing around the hood was true, he was only fucking with her because that light-skinned bitch didn't want his ass no more.

"Yeah, girl. My baby daddy must've known shit was going to pop off. You know he would lose his mind if anything ever happened to me or Karson," I told her.

She didn't need to know that Myeke wasn't fucking with me, and she damn sure didn't need to know that I was the one that helped set him up. Monica was my friend, and I loved the girl to death, but wasn't that much love in the world to make me tell her the truth. The bitch had loose lips, and I didn't need my ship sunk no fucking time soon.

"See, that's what me and bae need. I just know he gon' cash out on me and his baby."

"Bitch, are you believing your own lie now? You lied to that man and told him that you were pregnant," I reminded her.

Monica had to be delusional. You could only pull off a fake pregnancy for so long because sooner or later, you gotta start gaining weight or produce a baby, and that bitch couldn't do either one.

"It was a lie at first, but now I really am pregnant. I took a test this morning," she admitted.

My mouth dropped because I couldn't believe this bitch had actually trapped him. I may not have liked O'Hajee's rude ass, but I wouldn't want no nigga to get trapped with Monica as a baby mama. The bitch looked nice on paper, but I knew the truth. She was a bum ass bitch that didn't want shit out of life but to get pregnant by a hood nigga and become hood royalty. But hell, I wanted the same thing, so I couldn't talk. Shit, birds of a feather.

"Damn, bitch. Is it even his baby?" I asked.

"To his knowledge it is, so that's all that matters," she replied nonchalantly, and all I could do was shake my head.

This bitch was scandalous, but if she liked it, then I loved it. I wasn't knocking her hustle.

"You ain't shit."

"Neither are you. But enough about me; when are you coming back to NY? You know I ain't got shit to do when you not around."

"Girl, I don't even know. I'm just waiting on my baby to call me and tell me it's safe for us to come back. I'm just sad that he won't let me come visit him while he in the hospital," I told her.

"That's so fucked up, but at least he knows you safe. You lucky as hell because that man loves your dirty drawers," she said.

"You right about that," I replied.

Thinking about Myeke, I had to admit that I had a good nigga, but I fucked that up. I couldn't even say that I wasn't regretting the shit, but it didn't matter now. I knew that I couldn't go back to New York, without him or Deuce killing me for my betrayal. I wasn't sure which I was afraid of more, but for right now, Brooklyn was the last damn thing on my mind.

I talked to Monica on the phone for at least twenty more minutes before promising to call her later on in the week, and telling her to ask O'Hajee about Myeke for me before we hung up the phone, and I was left alone with my thoughts.

I could relax while I was here at Sydney's house, but I knew eventually she would start asking questions that I wasn't ready to answer. At a time like this, I was glad that I kept my family away from Myeke. They knew about him, but he didn't know anything about them. A part of me always knew that I would fuck up when it came to Key, and I would have to disappear for a little while, but I never imagined that I would fuck up this bad.

Now, not only was my life in danger, but everyone I was in contact with. But if I had to go down, I was all for taking these motherfuckas with me. All was fair in love and war, and I wouldn't be the only one losing in the end.

CHAPTER EIGHT

Emily James

$\mathcal{D}$oing the last of my rounds, I walked up and down the hallway before making my way to Myeke's room. Smoothing my hair up into its bun and rubbing my finger across my teeth, I straightened myself up before realizing that I was losing my mind.

Myeke was my patient, but over the past two weeks that he had been awake, I found myself going to his room a lot more than my other patients. If I wasn't helping him walk to therapy on the first floor, I was taking him to see Zoie while she was still here, or checking in on him during my lunch breaks. I knew I could get myself in trouble for spending so much time with a patient, but he was growing on me.

Knocking lightly on the door, I didn't wait for a response before stepping in the room, and the first face I saw was his. My breath got caught in my throat when the smirk spread across his face when he saw me standing in the doorway.

"I'm sorry. Am I interrupting?" I asked.

"Nah. Come in, Doc. Al was just helping me get these bags

together," he told me.

"Oh, right. Tomorrow's release day. I know you're happy to be getting out of here."

"Happy and sad."

"Why sad?" I asked, scrunching my face up a little.

"Because I won't get to see your pretty face every day," he replied.

I could feel my cheeks getting hot, and even though I should have told him it was inappropriate to flirt with me, I just smiled back and self-consciously played with my curly sideburns.

"Well, I'm sad to see you go as well, but it's a good thing. I just wanted to check in with you as well since you will be gone before my shift starts. I was trying to see if you had any questions or concerns before you were discharged."

"Boss man, I'ma get outta here. I'll be back to get you first thing in the morning," Al spoke up and told Key before he had a chance to respond to what I had said.

"Say less," Myeke replied, dapping him up before Al disappeared out the room, leaving the two of us alone.

Bouncing from one foot to the other, this was the first time I had been completely alone with him the whole time he was here and, for some reason, I was nervous as hell.

"Why you way over there? You can sit down. I'on bite." He smiled.

"I doubt that." I smirked, but against my better judgment, I walked over and took a seat on the end of his hospital bed. "I see you found some clothes to put on. You clean up nice," I commented.

Nice wasn't the word I wanted to use. Even though the nurses probably wouldn't agree with his attire, I felt like it was okay. He was dressed down in some denim Balmain jeans, a white V-neck that clung to his hard chest, and some all-white Jordans adorned his feet.

His wild curly hair was all over his head, and a part of me just wanted to reach out and touch it to see how soft it was.

"Yeah, a nigga got tired of walkin' around in that thin ass hospital gown. Had my ass all out," he joked, and I laughed because I had caught that sight a couple times when he was coming back in the room from going to use the bathroom.

"You need help." I laughed.

"Moms be saying the same shit. Like a nigga just throwed off or something."

"I could see that." I nodded.

"Oh yeah? What else could you see?" he asked, looking me in the eyes.

Staring back at him, I tried to swallow the lump that had formed in my throat, and I had to wipe my sweaty hands on my dress pants. I wasn't scheduled to do any surgeries today, so I opted out of wearing my scrubs to work, but I kept some in my office at all times, just in case of emergencies.

"Key, you're my patient," I told him.

"Not as of tomorrow morning. Hell, as of tonight when you clock out. I know the shit ain't ideal, but I know you feeling a nigga," he commented.

"And how would you know that?" I asked, folding my arms across my chest.

"Because I see the way you look at a nigga when you think he ain't looking. You blush when I smirk at you, and you always play in your hair when I compliment you. If you think I'm an ugly nigga, just let me know, and I'll try to fall back."

"*Try?*" I repeated.

"Yeah, try. I ain't makin' no promises, because I'm a man that believes in going after what he wants."

"And what exactly is it that you want?"

"You," he replied, pointing at me.

Every voice in my head was telling me to run in the other direction and to get out of this room with him, but curiosity was making me stay. Like, you know how you probably shouldn't go near a beehive, but you want the honey, so you ignore all warning signs? That was what was happening right now, and I wasn't trying to get stung, but I couldn't convince myself to walk away.

"But why me?"

"Shit, why not you?" He shrugged. "I'ma keep it real wit you, Doc. A nigga young, wild, and a little reckless at times, but my heart made of gold. I love hard, and I know I ain't perfect, but I'll always try to be. I'll always do my best to protect your heart, and I'll never intentionally hurt you.

I know you wondering where this could go and hell, me too. It may not go past this room, or I could be ya nigga for the rest of ya life.

You'll never know unless you gimme a chance," Myeke told me, and even though his delivery was all crazy, I believed him.

"I don't know what to say," I admitted.

"Don't say anything. Just give me your number and have an open mind. The shit is a little unorthodox, I know, but as long as you gimme a chance, I'll rock wit' you."

Nodding my head, I pulled out a pen and wrote my number in the corner of the papers I had drawn up for him to take with him when he left; a list of what to do and not to do while his body was still healing.

Handing the papers over to him, I stood to my feet and looked down at him.

"I've never done this before," I told him.

"Me neither, but rock wit' the kid, and you'll see," he told me, standing to his feet.

Pulling me into his arms, he kissed the top of my forehead, and I melted in his embrace.

"On the real though, thank you, ma. I could've been six feet under by now had it not been for you."

"I was just doing my job."

"I appreciate it either way."

Pulling back some, I looked up at him with a smile on my face and noticed that he had one on his as well, staring back down into my eyes. Without warning, he leaned down and softly pressed his lips against mine, and I swear I felt electricity race through my body. His lips were just as soft as they looked. I should've pulled away, but I didn't, as I stood on my tiptoes and deepened the kiss.

Snaking his tongue in and out of my mouth, his lips caressed and made love to my mouth, causing my panties to get soaked in a matter of seconds. Gripping my lower back, he pulled my body closer to his hard chest, and I started to get light headed. Pulling back, embarrassed, I took a step back and looked into his hooded eyes as he bit his bottom lip.

"I'm sorry. I shouldn't have done that," I whispered.

Not waiting on him to say anything, I turned on my heels to walk out of the room, but just as I got to the door to open it, he placed a hand on the door to keep it closed and wrapped his other arm around my waist.

"Don't apologize when it's something you want," he whispered in my ear. "Never hold back wit' me, ma. Okay?"

Nodding my head up and down to let him know I heard him, I refused to use my voice, afraid of what I might say, but I heard him loud and clear.

"Good," he said, kissing my neck and backing away from me so that I could open the door.

Looking back over my shoulder, he was still a few feet away with that cocky lopsided smirk that I was beginning to love so much. Turning back around, I opened the door and damn near ran out of his room to put some distance between us. I was hot and bothered, and I knew that my bullet would be put to good use as soon as I got home, thinking about the kiss that we just shared and the way his lips felt pressed against my neck.

I wasn't sure what I was thinking by giving him my phone number, but I knew that getting mixed up with Myeke could potentially be bad for my health. However, I didn't care one way or another. This could be something great or something bad, but I wanted to see where this went. No, I had to see where this went, and I wouldn't be satisfied until I did. I just prayed that he kept his word and didn't hurt me, because I didn't think I could handle that heartbreak.

CHAPTER NINE

O'Hajee

Jumping out of my sleep, I looked around the dark room, covered in sweat. Looking over at my watch, I saw it was a quarter to three in the morning, and I was having that damn nightmare again.

Laying back down, I laid on my back, staring into the dark, trying to catch my breath and get my heart rate under control. I hadn't had nightmares since I was seven, and now here I am damn near twenty years old, having them every night. Sometimes twice a night.

The night after I took Zoie to the hospital, I went back to her crib to see what the fuck happened only to find her room trashed and her sheets on her bed covered in blood, cum, and piss. Seeing that shit brought me to my knees. I broke down so bad and vowed to gut whoever did this shit to her. I remembered her telling me that she had money saved up one night we were talking, so I started looking for it to get it out the apartment for her, only to find out that it was already gone.

It took me about thirty minutes to pack up all her stuff and take it to my apartment. I packed her a small bag to keep at the hospital for when she woke up, but I'd be damned if she stepped foot back in that apartment. The guilt ate away at me because she was only in that place because I was ignoring her. I couldn't handle it.

I let my guilt for me selling her mom drugs, in the beginning, push me to the point that I couldn't be around her, knowing her home position. She never spoke on any sexual abuse going on, but if them niggas was that bold to fuck with her now, I'm sure it had happened before, and it fucked me up that she didn't tell a nigga about it. I would've handled the situation differently.

But I couldn't be on no could've, should've, would've. All I could do now was make sure I kept my word to her from here on out. I failed her once, and I refused to do the shit again. Once my breathing was under control, I sat back up in the bed and went to relieve my bladder before washing my hands and heading into the kitchen to grab a bottle of water.

Rounding the corner, I saw my mom sitting at the kitchen table, smoking a cigarette. Grabbing my water, I sat down on the other side and took a sip as she stared at me.

"What you doin' up, ol' lady?" I joked.

"Boy, I'll show you old," she said, pointing her cigarette at me. "I heard you screaming in your sleep. Thought someone was in here."

"I was not screaming."

"Could've fooled me. What's goin' on wit' you? And don't say nothin'."

Blowing out a breath of frustration, I wiped the sweat off my face and thought about all the shit that was on my mind. I didn't know where to start, but I knew she wasn't just going to drop the subject. She knew about Zoie, and she knew that me and Myeke were not speaking, but she didn't know about me killing Sac. I wasn't sure if I should tell her, but I needed to tell someone before I lost my fucking mind.

"Whatever you thinkin' about not telling me, that's where you need to start because it must be the most important," she said, pulling me out of my thoughts.

She used to do the same shit when I was a kid. I learned that she knew me better than I knew myself, and I could never get away with shit. I guess that shit didn't go away just because I got older.

"I killed him, Ma," I whispered, looking down at my hands.

"Say that again."

"I killed him, Ma," I repeated. This time I knew she heard me clear because she stood up walked over to me.

Without saying anything, she wrapped her arms around me and rubbed my back. I wasn't sure how I felt, but there was something in me that was eating me up about killing Sac. I felt no remorse about what I did, and I didn't think twice about pulling the trigger, but there was something in my conscious that just wouldn't let me get over it.

I may mule drugs, but I wasn't no killer, and my mind was trying to remind me of that shit every time I closed my eyes. My mom rocked me in her arms for a good ten minutes, just whispering and rubbing her hands through my hair.

"Did it have something to do wit' what's going on with you and your brother?" she finally asked.

"Yeah," I replied, nodding my head.

"Friend?"

"Nah," I answered, shaking my head.

"Then we never talk about this again," she told me, and I nodded my head in agreement.

"Look at me, O'Hajee," she commanded, pulling away from me and grabbing my face in her hands. "I don't condone you killing anyone, but I will not lose another son. Whatever this is... whatever is eating away at you, I need you to bury it deep inside, baby, and push it to the back of your head. Do you hear me?"

"But Ma, how am I supposed to do that shit? I can't even get a full night's rest. My head always hurting from lack of sleep. I'm angry as fuck all the time, and I feel like I'm losing my mind," I admitted.

"I'ma let you slide with all the cussing because you're upset, but let that be the last time you cuss in my presence," she said, chastising me. "But you do whatever you gotta do, O'Hajee. You push it back there, and no matter how hard it tries to fight, you can't let it out. That girl needs you more now than she ever did before. She literally has nothing now, and even though your brother won't say it, he needs you too."

"Key ain't thinkin' about me." I scoffed, pushing away from her gently.

"Yes he is. Your brother is a lot of things, and the main one is stubborn, but he loves you. He's pissed that you did some shit that you had no business doing. Not only because you went behind his back, but because he could've lost you the same way he lost Rod.

I wasn't the best mother after your brother passed away. I left you two alone to not only deal with the death of your brother, but the pain of your father dying as well. I was weak, I shut down, and I did the one thing I felt could make me feel better, and I shouldn't have done that. Myeke sacrificed a lot to raise you in my absence, and he still feels that weight. No matter how old you get, he will always want to protect you, and whether you see it or not, Myeke feels like he failed you."

"That don't make no sense, Ma. I'm grown; I make my own decisions. Key didn't force me to get caught up. I wanted to get my own money and prove that I could stand on my own two feet. I was giving you money even when I knew what you would do with it and still letting Key pay bills here, even though I had the money.

That nigga was right, I am selfish, and I almost lost two of the people that I love the most behind my selfish ways. I can't lose them though, Ma. I think I'm going crazy now that both of them are mad at me. But what I'ma do if they wash they hands with me for real?" I asked.

"Quit thinking negative. The stuff with you and Myeke will pass, and you two will be thick as thieves again in no time. You just gotta give him his space and let him come to you. As for Zoie, I don't know what happened between the two of you, but that girl loves you as much as you love her," she told me.

"I messed up, Ma. I pushed her away, and now she don't even want to deal wit' me no more. Shorty was asking crazy questions, like can I give her virginity back and then she'll forgive me, but if I can't, to stay away from her. What kind of shit is that?"

"What made you push her away? I thought y'all were fine," she asked.

"We are. I mean we were, until the night of her graduation. I realized who her mom was."

"And?"

"Back when I first thought I wanted to sell drugs, I was actually slanging rocks. A man came to me and asked could he grab a vial of crack. Her mom was with him. She looked iffy about it at first, but after he pulled out a rock and smoked it, he passed it to her, and she hit it. I'm the reason that her moms is even on that shit. How could I look her in the face knowing that?" I questioned more to myself than to her.

Ever since the day her mom came in to her graduation acting an ass, I felt like shit. I watched her mom take that first hit, and I was the one that handed it to them.

"You can't blame yourself for that, O'Hajee. You didn't put that crack pipe to her lips and make her smoke it. That is a grown ass woman, and she was going to do it regardless. If it wasn't you that sold it to her, she would've gotten it from somewhere else," she explained.

"But it was me, Ma. I couldn't handle the guilt."

"Well too damn bad! You got a beautiful girl that needs you, and you gon' hold back from her all because her mother wants to be a crackhead?"

When she said it like that, it didn't make any sense for me not to deal with Zoie, but a part of me was afraid that she wouldn't forgive me for the role I played in it, and then another part was screaming for me to tell her because I needed my baby back in my life.

"Yeah, aight. I'ma fix it," I said, finally responding to her.

"You better. Now let me get back in here and try to get some sleep, and remember what I said, O'Hajee. Push it to the back of your mind. You need to get some sleep."

"Yes, ma'am."

"Okay, baby. Goodnight. I love you."

"Love you too, Ma," I replied, standing to my feet and kissing her on the forehead.

Turning out the kitchen light, we both walked down the hallway toward our rooms. Stopping in front of my door, I called out to her just before she could close it all the way.

"Yo, Ma?"

"Huh?"

"Why'd you stop? What changed?" I asked.

My mom had been home for weeks and I hadn't seen her sniff a line. She chain smoked the hell out of cigarettes, but that was about it. Come to think about it, I hadn't seen her in weeks before she showed back up acting normal again. I wasn't complaining, but I was curious.

"I did," was all she said before closing her door.

Walking back in the room, I changed the sweat drenched sheets and started remaking my bed, thinking about the conversation we had. Once I was done, I did something I hadn't done in a long time. I got on my knees and prayed. I prayed for everything that happened, everything that was to come. Instead of asking him to take it all away and make it stop, I asked him to make me a stronger man to deal with all the drama that I caused in my life.

To give me strength for everything that was to come because I knew it was far from over. Getting back in the bed, I did exactly what my mom said and pushed it all into the furthest corner of my mind I could find, and closed my eyes. Before I realized it, my mind was clear, and I fell into the deepest sleep that I'd had in weeks.

* * *

Waking up a few hours later, I decided to throw on some dark denim jeans that hung off my waist, a mint green Lacoste shirt, and a pair of crisp white Forces. I wasn't trying to overdo it, but I knew I wanted to look good for my lil' mamas.

Zoie was set to get out of the hospital today, and even though she wasn't feeling me right now, I kept my word and had been stopping by to see her every day. Her doctor let it slip that she was getting out today, and I was going to make sure that I was there to help her out.

Making sure I had everything, I grabbed my wallet, car keys, and my phone, and I was out the door. After finding out that Monica was pregnant, I let her get the car back and went out and got me a 2015 Chevy Malibu. I paid for it flat out because I didn't have time to pay no car note every month. Hopping behind the wheel, I put the car in drive and headed to the hospital.

Thinking about all the bad that was surrounding us in Pink Houses, I started to think that Myeke had the right idea about moving out, and I was going to start looking into some places once I was home and got Zoie settled. Since the day she had gone off on the caseworker about being put into the system for four months, I hadn't heard nothing else about it, but I'd rather her be safe than sorry.

So, first thing in the morning, I was taking her to the courthouse to do that emancipation shit she was talking about. I was so caught up in my thoughts that my normal twenty-five-minute drive was cut down to fifteen. Parking my car close to the entrance, I jumped out and hit the alarm before going inside and taking the elevator up to the second floor.

The whole way to her room, I started to get nervous, and my heart started beating out of my chest. Zoie wasn't playing with me at all, so I knew the moment I walked in the door, her attitude was going to be on ten-thousand, but if that's what it took to get back in her good graces, then I was all for it.

I took a deep breath and pushed the door open without knocking. Not seeing her sitting on the bed, I walked further in, just as she was coming around the corner with her overnight bag in her hand.

"Where you goin'?"

"Away from you. Now, if you would just move," she said kissing her teeth.

"Bro, chill wit' all that. Do we gotta beef every time I come up here?"

"Nope, because I'm no longer staying here, so you'll be here by yourself. Move."

When she tried to step around me, I moved in her way and did it three more times until she finally got annoyed and pushed me.

"Move, O'Hajee!" she snapped.

"Oh, you mad?" I teased with a smirk on my face.

"Do you gotta be so immature?"

"Do you gotta be so mean?" I asked.

"Do you gotta be a cheater?" she shot back with a grimace on her face.

"Yo, ma. You draggin' it right now. This what we on? I thought we was better than that, lil' mamas."

"Yeah. Me too," she sassed, rolling her eyes again.

Biting on my bottom lip, I started thinking back to the days that she would walk by me in the courtyard, and I would bother her just to get under her skin, and this time was no different. I wanted to get back in her good graces, but she made it too easy to fuck with her. Her emotions be written all over her face.

Just like now. She was barking all that tough tony shit, but her body language told me she wanted me there, and the lust behind her eyes told me that she missed me in more ways than one.

"C'mon, ma. Let daddy make it better," I whispered, taking a step closer to her.

Backing up, she started shaking her head from side to side until she walked into the bed and was forced to sit down. Gently pushing her shoulder, I laid on top of her, careful not to put my weight on her, as I looked into her eyes.

Pushing her curly hair out of her face, I stared at her and saw everything I wanted for the rest of my life. A nigga messed up, but I couldn't lose my heart behind that shit. No matter what she said, the shit wasn't happening. I'd kidnap her ass first.

"You gotta let me make it right, ma," I whispered, nuzzling my nose into the side of her neck.

"I don't have to do anything. Get off me, Hajee, you're heavy," she whined, but didn't put up too much of a fight.

"I'll let you up when you tell me that you'll give me a chance."

"Aren't you tired of me saying no?"

"Aren't you tired of telling me no? Look, you can answer my question, or I can keep you pinned down on this bed. The choice is yours. I got all day," I told her, kissing her jawline.

Rolling her eyes up into her head, she huffed but didn't say anything. Damn near five minutes passed by before her stubborn ass finally spoke up again.

"Fine! Just get your heavy ass off me. My legs are goin' numb," she snapped.

Grinning like the Cheshire cat, I got off her and pulled her to her feet and into my arms.

"I promise you won't regret this, ma."

"Oh, I know I won't," she replied. "I said that I would give you a chance. Never said we were back together, my nigga."

"How I'm supposed to fix shit if we ain't together?" I griped.

"Not my problem. And I'm hungry."

"I'll get you whatever you want."

"Anything I want?" she asked, turning to look at me.

"Anything."

"I want Chipotle."

"Alright. Let's go."

"Grab my bag and follow me, or I will leave you in your car," she told me.

"How you gon' leave me and I got the keys?" I asked.

Holding up her left hand, she jingled my car keys in front of me with that sexy smirk on her face. She straight lifted my keys out my pocket, and I didn't even know it. Reaching out to grab them, she kept them out of arm's reach and took a step back.

"Uh-uh. You gotta be quicker than that." She laughed. "Now c'mon or get left," she threw over her shoulder as she opened the door and walked out of the room.

"Yes, ma'am." I smirked, following her out the room.

Yeah. Wasn't no way I was letting her go. Zoie was stuck with me until death do us part, and I didn't even think she realized it yet.

CHAPTER TEN

Myeke

"Come on, Mr. Compton, just one more." The therapist coached me as I tried to lift the dumbbell.

The pain that shot through my chest and my arm was damn near unbearable, but I wouldn't let him know that. Ever since I'd been shot, I was having to learn simple shit all over again. I lived in the gym because I had one in my house, but now, I could barely do three reps with twenty-pound dumbbells.

Doing the last set, I dropped them on the floor and blew out a breath of frustration. I wasn't feeling this shit at all, but if this was the only way I could get back in the streets heavy without getting winded or being weak, then this was what I would do.

"Good job, Mr. Compton. How are you feeling?"

"I'm recovering from getting shot. How the fuck do you think I feel?" I barked.

It wasn't his fault, but he wanted to ask stupid questions, so I was gon' give his ass a stupid answer.

"Myeke," I heard Em chide from across the room.

Looking over my shoulder, I hit her with a wink and looked back at the therapist.

"My bad."

"It's quite alright. I'm getting used to it now." He shrugged. "We're all done for today. I'll see you Friday around the same time."

"Cool," I replied, taking a sip of my water.

"And don't worry; I'll let myself out. See you later, Dr. James."

"You too, Byron," she replied with a wave.

Swaggering over to where she sat on the bench, I stopped in front of her and just stared. It had been a week since I got released and she gave me her number. I wasted no time hitting her up, and that night, we talked on the phone for hours like we were two teenagers, until we fell asleep. The next day, I popped up on her at work to take her to lunch, and we'd been seeing each other every day since.

"Do you have to be so rude to everyone, Myeke?" she asked, standing on her feet.

"I'm not rude. This just my mouth," I replied with a shrug.

"You say that, but I've seen you be nice before."

"Oh, yeah? To who?"

"Me." She smiled.

"You don't count. I gotta be nice to you. You can kill me in my sleep or some shit. Have motherfuckas thinkin' a nigga died of natural causes and shit," I joked.

Laughing, she punched me in the chest, and I winced instinctively. Her hands flew to her mouth.

"I am so sorry. I forgot," she apologized. "Let me check to make sure I didn't pop a stitch. You also need to change the dressing on these. Especially since you've been sweating."

"You gon' do it for me?"

The question wasn't sexual at all, but I dropped my voice and looked at her with such intensity that she started to blush and shift from one foot to the next. Smirking down at her, I didn't think I would ever get use to the way her body reacted to me, and I hadn't even touched her yet. Other than the day in the hospital, I hadn't even kissed her.

I overstepped a little bit, and though we were kicking it, I wanted her to get to know the real me, and I wanted to do the same with her. I knew that sex would only complicate shit between us.

"Um, I can," she said, clearing her throat.

"Say less. Let me hop in the shower and then I'll let you handle that."

"Okay."

Kissing her on the forehead, I walked out my gym and headed up the stairs toward my room. When I made it to the top of the stairs, I instinctively looked over toward Karson's room like I did every night. Just looking at the empty room, a wave of anger and sadness washed over me, and the reality that I hadn't seen or heard from my son in weeks, hit me.

I had never been away from Karson since the day he was born, and now that I was, the shit had me anxious. I hadn't seen or heard from Siya since the night she called my phone telling me that Karson was having trouble breathing. I knew now that it was a lie, but I still wanted to lay eyes on him to see for myself.

I had never been the type to kill women, but when I got my hands on Siya's ass, I wasn't sure what I was liable to do to her. She had to be planning this for a minute because the safe in my room was wiped clean, and all of their clothes were gone. Like she knew that she wasn't coming back. But what she should have made them do was made sure that I was dead before they walked away.

Nothing on this Earth could save them from the shit that I had planned. I didn't know how she linked up with Deuce, but when I got ahold to him, it was over with. No talking. No questions. No playing. That nigga had to get it, but before he died, he would feel every bullet that I felt the night he tried to kill me.

Closing Karson's door, I went into my room and started the shower. Afterward, I took all the bandages off my chest and stripped out of my clothes, before stepping in the shower. Letting the water fall over my body, I wet my hair and started to wash my body, careful not to rub my scars too hard.

Once I was done, I dried off and wrapped a towel around my hair and my lower body. Settling on a pair of gray sweets, I slid them on before grabbing a pair of socks and walking back downstairs to see what Emily was up to.

Walking back into the living room, I saw that she had everything she needed to patch me back up. Shorty was the truth for real, and I had no plans on letting her get away from me any time soon.

"You do know that your skin needs to be dry in order for the bandages to stick, right?" Emily asked with a raised eyebrow.

"Chill. I got you covered," I replied as I pulled the towel off of my hair.

My curly damp hair fell to my shoulders, and the look on her face let me know that she approved of it. Most dudes with hair kept theirs braided, but I kept my hair in its natural curly state. Niggas that didn't know me mistook it for me being a pretty nigga that was softer than cotton, but when I let that gun clap, they realized the error of their ways before they took their last breath.

"Thank you," she said, taking the towel out of my hand. "Sit, please."

"Yes, ma'am."

Sitting down on the couch, I watched her every move as she dried my chest as gently as she could, before starting the process of putting the bandages back and wrapping my chest. The look of intensity on her face caused my dick to brick up in my sweats. I guess the movement caught her eye because she looked down and her eyes grew as wide as saucers.

"Oh my God! I am so sorry," she yelped, jumping up.

"My bad, shorty. Let me go put some boxers on. I ain't mean to scare you. My mans just got a mind of his own," I said, trying not to laugh at her reaction.

Shorty was acting like she had never seen a dick before. I'm sure being a doctor, she saw all types of dicks. But a nigga was blessed, so I was used to the reaction. I could've had my fair share of females, but I was loyal to Siya. Even if the bitch wasn't shit.

"It's… Um, it's okay," she murmured, clearing her throat. "I just haven't seen someone so… blessed."

"Damn, shorty. Them niggas you been fuckin' wit' must not got shit to show."

"It's not that. You must think that's normal?" she asked, gesturing towards my dick.

"I mean. I'on know about normal, but trust, I don't go around lookin' at other niggas' dicks. My shit is my shit, and theirs is theirs. I just know a nigga is 'blessed' as you call it," I told her, smirking.

Now that her embarrassment had worn off, she was staring in amazement like she wasn't sure if she should run or ask if she could ride it. I was cool with the latter, but I would never make the first move unless she showed me that's what she wanted.

Emily was bad as hell, and the fact that she was a single surgeon, with a good head on her shoulders and no kids, had me ready to lock her down before someone else realized how precious she was.

"Why you lookin' at me like that, ma? You see somethin' you want?" I asked.

"I'm sorry," she replied, her cheeks turning red as hell. "You can go change now," she told me, but she kept stealing glancing at it.

Instead of walking away, I closed the distance between us and took her hand in mine. Putting her hand on the part of my chest that she hadn't bandaged yet, I let her run her hands across it until she got to my abs and close to the waistband of my sweats.

"Pull it out," I told her, and she looked up at me with shock written all over her face.

"Key, I don't know if—"

"I didn't say you had to do anything wit' it. I just said pull it out. You keep lookin' at it through the fabric, and I can tell you curious, so this is your free pass," I explained.

She stood there for a second looking unsure of herself, but letting her hand linger around my v-cut. I still hadn't figured out why, but that shit always made my dick brick up ten times harder when a female ran her fingertips along that line, and the fact that she was doing it, had my shit ready to break free.

Placing my hand on top of hers, I guided it inside my pants and wrapped her small hand around my dick and let her hand go.

"Now it's all up to you."

The lust that ran through her eyes caused my dick to jump, and she squeezed it lightly before doing like I originally commanded and pulled it out completely. My face held a lopsided smile because I could damn near hear the dirty thoughts that were running through her head.

"It's beautiful," she whispered, never looking up at me.

"I'on know about all that shit, but it's a dick." I shrugged.

What she did next surprised the hell out of me. I watched as she got on her knees and looked back up at me for approval while she glided her small hands up and down the shaft of my dick. Biting my bottom lip, I nodded my head up and down, and that was all the confirmation she needed before taking the tip in her mouth and covering it with spit.

It took her a few tries to fit all of it in her mouth, but once she found a good rhythm, that was all it took. The way she was bobbing, sucking, and slobbing on my dick had me curling my toes so hard, them bitches popped.

"Shitttt, girlll," I hissed.

It was taking everything in me not to fuck her face. They said them good girls are freaks, but damn! I let her suck me up for a good five minutes before I couldn't handle it no more. I was never the type to nut off head. Yeah, the shit felt amazing, but it just wasn't for me. But the way she had my balls tightening up had me ready to introduce her tonsils to all my future kids.

Trying not to be rough with her, I put my hands in her hair and guided my dick in and out her mouth, bringing my nut to the tip. When I felt myself about to nut, I tried to pull my dick out, but she wasn't hearing that shit at all. She placed her hand on my hips and held on as I shot my nut down her throat.

"Fuckkkkkkk!" I growled, watching her drain my shit as she looked up into my eyes.

Standing to her feet, she wiped the sides of her mouth as that same embarrassed look covered her face again. I could tell that she wasn't used to doing shit like that, but I wasn't complaining.

"I shouldn't have—" She started to apologize, but the force of my lips crashing into hers stopped her.

I was full of firsts today because I never allowed Siya to kiss me after she swallowed my nut. I always thought that was like me sucking my own dick, but with Em, I couldn't help that shit. My dick was still hard as hell, and I needed to relieve this pressure.

"Take this shit off," I demanded, breaking our kiss.

She wasn't moving fast enough for me, so once she got her shirt over her head, I pushed her back on the couch and damn near ripped her pants from her body. If I wasn't in such a hurry, I would've taken a second to admire the all-black lace bra and panty set she had on, but we had later for that. I needed to see what I was getting myself into.

True, I was feeling her, but I had to test drive it first. I couldn't cuff a bitch with mediocre pussy. Hell, I may cheat for the first time in my life if that was the case.

Sliding her panties down, I dropped to my knees so that I was hovering over her. Her lips were fat as hell, and I could tell that she got them waxed because the smoothness spoke for itself. There wasn't a hair in sight.

Reaching my arm behind her, I unhooked her bra with one hand and pulled it off to let her C-cups free. Everything about her was perfect, and if I was a weak man, I would've bust all over myself and hadn't even felt her yet.

"If you don't want to do this, ma, speak now or forever hold your peace because once I start, I won't be able to stop," I admitted.

"I want to. You just have to be gentle. It's been awhile," she confessed, slightly embarrassed.

"What's a while? Like six months?"

"More like six years."

"Six years? How old are you again?"

"Twenty-eight."

"And you haven't had sex in six years." It was a question, but it came off more as a statement than anything.

"I haven't had sex since my first boyfriend. I can still count on my hands how many times I've had sex," she replied.

"Say less. I got you," I told her before putting my hands on her waist and pulling her to the edge of the couch.

Hearing that she hadn't been touched in six years and it was only by one man, had a nigga hyped as hell. It was rare as fuck to find women like her, and I was prepared to show her what she had been missing.

Lifting her butt up slightly off the couch, I leveled her pussy with my mouth before going to work. I wasn't gon' flex and say I didn't like it because I loved eating pussy. It was something about it, and Emily's was so good that I could eat her shit for hours. It had a sweet smell to it, and the taste was even better.

"Ooouuu," she cried out, rocking her hips.

"That's right, baby. Fuck daddy's face," I said, coaxing her.

Latching onto her clit, I slurped, sucked, and tongue fucked her until she was squirming in my hands trying to break free from the assault I was delivering to her. I watched the way her eyes rolled to the back of her head, and the look of her pleasure on her face made me go harder.

Thirty seconds later, her body started to shake, and her juices shot out of her, wetting my chin, lips, and my nose. Refusing to stop, I latched my tongue on her clit and kept sucking until her body stopped shaking and she looked spent.

"Uh-uh, shorty. You can't tap out on me yet. I got too much planned for you," I told her, sliding her body off the couch and placing the head of my dick at her opening before gently sliding her down on to me.

Trying to ease the discomfort I knew she was feeling, I began to kiss on her neck, careful not to leave passion marks. Moaning, she threw her head back as her walls opened up to me, allowing me to slide all the way in. Sitting still for a moment, I let her adjust to my size before I started moving her up and down on my dick so that she could catch her own pace.

When she did, that was all she wrote. For the rest of the night, we sucked and fucked each other until we were both spent. By the time it was all over and done with, we were butt ass naked, laid out on my living room floor. In this moment, life was perfect… well, almost.

CHAPTER ELEVEN

O'Hajee

The constant buzzing of my phone on my dresser caused me to stir in my sleep. Looking over to my left, I saw that Zoie was still in my bed sleeping. After we left the hospital, we went out to eat, and even though she called herself having an attitude with me at first, she finally loosened up, and shit seemed normal between us.

We laughed, joked, and just spent time with each other until we laid in the bed talking until we both passed out. She didn't mention what happened to her, and I didn't mention what happened between me and Monica. I knew that we would eventually have to talk about it because we couldn't avoid the topics forever, but for now, I was okay with us being back to normal.

Watching her sleep for a few more seconds, I admired her beauty, pushing her hair to the side so that I could see her beautiful face. She still had a few bruises on her face, but they didn't take away from her beauty. They were beginning to lighten up, and I could tell they would be completely gone in a couple weeks. My lil' mamas was just breathtaking, and a nigga was lucky as hell to have her.

My staring was short lived because my phone started buzzing again on the dresser, pulling me out of my daydreams. Easing out the bed, careful not to wake her, I silenced it before stepping into the hallway to see who it was. Seeing Monica's name flash across my screen, I ran my hand down my face while blowing out a breath of frustration, before sliding the cursor across the phone to answer it.

"Yeah?" I answered, looking over my shoulder to make sure Zoie hadn't woken up.

"Yeah? What the fuck do you mean yeah, O'Hajee? What's up wit' you? We been inseparable for the past couple weeks, but now you treating me like I don't exist. What's up with that?" she barked into the phone.

"Chill, B. We weren't inseparable. You came over here and never left. Hell, I gave you the car for you to be able to drive yourself home, and you still didn't leave. Look, Monica, what happened was a mistake. I was going through some shit, and a nigga was weak for letting you top me off. I should've stopped you, but I didn't.

That shit on me, but you knew just as well as I did that I got a girl. Shit, one that I love, and I fucked up. Shit, you know all about her the way that she smacked yo' ass for disrespecting her," I told her.

"Oh, so you back wit' that bitch? That's what the fuck this is about? I'm having your baby, and you throw me to the side for that bitch?" she had the nerve to ask.

Pulling my phone away from my ear, I looked at it like she could see me before putting it back to my ear.

"Let that be the last time you disrespect my girl to me. Her smacking yo' ass is goin' to be the least of your worries, my nigga, and I put that shit on yo' life," I warned. "As far as you being pregnant wit' my baby, shorty, you tried it. I ain't never ran up in you raw. This last time was a fuckin' mistake, but you can believe that shit will never happen again."

"You say that now, Hajee, but we both know that you can't resist this pussy. You will be back. You always are," she shot back.

"Shorty, you draggin' it. Ain't nobody worried about you or that tired ass pussy, son."

"I bet my pussy is better than your bitch's."

Feeling myself get heated, I pinched the bridge of my nose, ready to go off on her ass, when I felt someone tap me on my shoulder. Turning around, I came face to face with an annoyed Zoie, and I felt my heart drop to my stomach. I wasn't sure how much she heard, but from the look on her face, I can tell that it was enough.

Not saying a word, she held her hand out, reaching for my phone. I could still hear Monica going in on the other end. She was calling me all kinds of bum ass niggas and telling me how I wasn't shit, but none of that shit mattered. I was just afraid of what Zoie was about to do with my ass. She had murder in her eyes.

Relaxing her face, she grabbed my phone before I could hand it to her and placed it to her ear.

"Look, if by some miracle your baby happens to be O'Hajee's, then he will handle his responsibility, but make this the last time that you call my man at seven in the morning, and him not wanting your dusty ass will be the least of your fuckin' worries. Now if you will excuse us, we're going back to sleep," Zoie told her in a calm tone before hanging up the phone.

Without another word, she placed it in my hand and walked away back toward my room, leaving me standing there stuck. It took me a few seconds to grasp what just happened, before Monica started calling my phone back to back.

Hitting ignore, I walked back in the room to see her sitting on the bed in the dark. Taking a deep breath, I braced myself before walking in and closing the door behind me.

"Zoie," I called out, but she raised her hand to cut me off.

"Silence your phone and get back in the bed," she said, never looking up at me.

Doing as I was told, I put my phone on do not disturb and slid back in the bed. Laying down on my chest, she didn't say anything, but I could feel her heart beating before I felt her warm tears hit my chest. Pulling her further into my arms, I held her while she cried.

"Please don't cry. I'm sorry. I fucked up. Just don't cry, ma," I pleaded.

"Why? Was it because of somethin' I did? Why did you leave me? I needed you." She sobbed, and my heart broke in my chest.

Pulling her body on top of mine, I leaned up and wrapped her legs around my waist carefully so I wouldn't hurt her. I looked into her eyes as she cried and did my best to dry them. I told her I would never be the cause of her pain, and I failed. I failed her in the worst way, but I couldn't have her blaming herself for my fuck up.

"No. Never let me hear me say that shit again. Nothing is wrong with you, Zoie. I fucked up. This all on me. Nothing that you could ever do should've resulted in the shit I did. You didn't deserve that shit, ma, and even if it takes me the rest of my life, I will make it up to you. You just gotta give me the chance to," I said.

"Then why?"

My head was screaming for me not to tell her the shit with her mom, but the conversation I had with my mom replayed in my head, and I knew that I owed her the truth, regardless of the consequences.

"I'll tell you everything. I just need you to stop cryin', baby. The shit breakin' my heart knowing this shit is my fault," I admitted.

Nodding her head, she tried her best to dry her tears, but I could see the shit was still taking a toll on her. She had been through hell, and I was supposed to be her safe haven, but with all the shit going on between us, I knew she couldn't even find that peace. She needed to know the truth. She deserved that much, considering the shit that I had done.

Once she calmed herself down enough, she looked at me, waiting for me to start talking. A few tears still cascaded down her cheeks, but she was visibly calmer, so I started talking.

"You remember the night of your graduation and your mom came in acting a fool?" I asked.

"Yeah. What about it?" she asked, nodding her head.

"You remember what you asked me later on that night at dinner?"

"Yeah. I asked were you embarrassed to be wit' me because you tensed beside me when you saw her."

"Yeah, and I told you no. I told you I could never be embarrassed to be with you regardless of who your parents were," I told her, causing her to smile a little. "I didn't tense up because I was embarrassed, ma. I tensed because I realized who your mom was," I confessed.

Hearing that, the smile dropped from her face and her body tensed up in my lap.

"So, you knew about what was happening to me in that house? Is that why you wanted to help me? You were just pitying me? Is that it?" she asked, firing off back to back questions.

"No, Zoie, no! If I would've known some foul shit was going on from that lady, no disrespect, but I would've put two in her head, and I wouldn't be having these fucked up nightmares afterwards like I been having," I told her.

"Wait, what nightmares?" she asked.

I had to smile myself because just that fast, she was no longer concerned about her. She heard that something was wrong with me, and she wanted to help me. She wanted to make me feel better, and that was one of the reasons that I loved her. She was selfless, and she had a heart made of gold.

"Focus, Zoie," I told her. "I noticed your mom because about six months back when I first got into selling, I thought that I could do the nickel and diming shit to make some money, ya know? One of my first sells was to this couple. A man and a woman. I could tell from jump that the dude had done it before, but not the lady.

She was hesitant at first, but after he promised to buy her a bottle if she just took a hit with him, she quickly agreed and took the crack pipe from him. I watched her light the glass vial on fire and take the hit before she looked me in my eyes. I watched her become a zombie almost instantly.

I told myself that day, I couldn't sling rocks because I would always remember the face of the lady that took that hit in front of me. I would see how it changed her and how she became a different person right before my eyes. That woman was your mom. I noticed that night when she showed up, and I started to feel guilty.

It's my fault that she hooked on crack now. I could've said something when the guy was telling her that she had to do it. I could've took the shit back and gave the money back, but I didn't. I just watched because I was curious. I had seen plenty of crackheads in my day, but I wanted to see how people made that decision from being clean to turning to full-blown junkies. I guess in a fucked-up way, I was trying to see what made my moms turn into that person overnight.

I couldn't tell you because I was scared of what you would do. I was the reason that your moms had took a turn for the worse. Because of me, she was this monster that I couldn't protect you from. I was scared that if you found out that it would break your heart and you'd hate me. So like a punk, I pushed you away, thinking that if you didn't love me anymore, it would make what I did easier, but that shit didn't help."

Telling her the truth lifted this weight off my shoulder, but the blank expression that she held on her face made me nervous all over again. I was expecting her to start screaming and curse me out and tell me she hated me and how I ruined her life. Knowing that the rape happened to her because of my actions fucked with me the most. All this time, I was afraid that I would lose her because of this shit, and the way things were looking, I was going to lose her anyway. Ain't that about a bitch?

"Say something," I told her after her just staring at me for five minutes.

"What do you want me to say?" she finally asked.

"Say something. Curse me out. Scream. Tell me you hate me. Tell me I ain't shit, but don't just not say anything. Your silence is worse. I need to know the damage I caused."

"It's fucked up, Hajee, and I could blame you for what you did, but that wouldn't do anything but make more excuses for her. Brenda is a grown ass woman, and she makes her own decisions. You may have sold them the crack, but you didn't put it to her lips and make her smoke it. She did that on her own.

After what happened that night, I watched the monster dance behind her eyes. She hates me. She always has. She allowed them to do this to me, and when I begged her to save me, she walked away. Nothing you did or didn't do could ever change that," she told me with a shrug of her shoulders.

"If this was a few weeks ago, you're right, I would've blamed you. I would've tried to put it off that the crack made her into this person, even though I would know in my heart that it wasn't true. I wouldn't have wanted to face reality. In a way, it's a good thing that you didn't tell me. I would've been still trying to protect her," she confessed, dropping her head. "I don't know what I ever did to make her hate me so much."

"Don't ever let me hear you say what happened to you was a good thing. No one deserves what you went through. I could've prevented all this shit if I would've told you. You would've been safe with me, but instead, you got assaulted because you went home," I said, getting pissed off all over again.

"Nothing you could've said or done would've prevented this. Mike finally got what he wanted. He always told me that he would. Only thing was, you got my virginity before he could," she said through her tears.

"Wait, this isn't the first time that this has happened?"

Dropping her head again, she shook her head 'no' and started to cry harder.

"Why didn't you tell me, baby? I would've never let you go back there. You would've been staying with me."

"I was scared. I didn't know how to tell you. I thought that if you knew all those things those men did to me and my body before I got my first period, you wouldn't want me. That you'd know I was tainted," she cried.

"How long has this been going on, Zoie?"

I wasn't sure why I asked, but I had to know. When she told me since she was eleven, my heart dropped. I listened to her cry and tell me everything that she'd endured from the time she was eleven years old. She told me about the first rape and the abuse. She told me about the first time she started boosting just so that her mom would stop selling her to random men. She wanted to make enough money to feed herself and feed her mom's habit.

By the time she got to the recent rape, we both had tears in our eyes. She cried as she explained the way they violated her, and all I saw was red. I didn't want to hear any more, but I could tell she needed to get the shit off her chest. I couldn't imagine what it was like carrying that shit around on her shoulders. To keep that shit bottled inside because she was afraid of what other people would think of her.

When she was done, she just lay in my arms crying until she cried herself to sleep. She held on to me for dear life, afraid of what would happen if she let me go. Laying back in the bed, I held her while she slept, thinking about all the shit that had happened in the past few weeks. I couldn't afford to take any more losses. Something had to give, and I knew where I needed to start first.

* * *

"Just go knock." Zoie coached me from the passenger seat.

I didn't respond to what she said; I just stared at Myeke's front door like it would automatically open by itself. Shit between us wasn't going to fix itself, and I missed my brother, but I wasn't about to beg his ass to start fucking with me again.

Zoie kept pressing, saying I needed to be the bigger person, and now here we were, sitting in his driveway. I wanted to turn back around and take my ass back to Pink Houses, but this was something I had to do, even if I didn't want to.

"Come on," I told her, getting out the car.

Waiting for her at the front of the car, I locked the doors and put her hand in mine.

"Myeke lives here by himself?" Zoie asked, looking at the house in amazement.

"Nah, he got his baby mama and my nephew Karson stayin' wit' him. You met him at your graduation, remember?"

"Yeah, but I didn't know they stayed together."

"Yep. Now come on. You acting like you ain't never seen a big house before, lil' nigga," I told her, walking up to the door.

"Son, we stay in the Pink Houses. Like the fuckin' gutta. Of course this shit is foreign to me. We not all used to havin' a kingpin for an older brother," she sassed, kissing her teeth.

"Don't let him hear you say that shit. That nigga head gon' get swole as a bitch," I told her as the door opened up.

Coming face to face with Dr. Emily, my eyebrows dipped because I just knew this nigga ain't sell his crib.

"Zoie. Hajee. I didn't know you guys were comin' over." She gasped, surprised, and I could tell she was a little embarrassed.

I already knew that the big t-shirt she had on belonged to Myeke because the nigga was infamous for those black V-necks. The shirt swallowed her little frame, as she stood in the doorway bouncing from foot to foot.

"Hell, I'm sure you didn't because if it was up to me, my ass wouldn't be here," I grumbled, cutting my eyes at Zoie.

"That was rude." Zoie chastised me, popping me in the back of my head and mugging me.

"You been around my moms too long. Keep hittin' on me and

I'ma jack ya lil' ass up," I told her.

"And I'll slap the hell out your big ass. Try me if you want to, and I'll grace ya ass wit' a buck fifty," she shot back with a smirk on her face.

"Oh, so you tough, lil' nigga?" I asked.

"Come and find out."

"Whoa, lil' sis. Don't be seducing this nigga on my front porch. You know a nigga got neighbors and shit," Myeke told her, coming around the corner, smiling.

He was shirtless, and his chest was bandaged up. His normal curly hair was all over his head, and he had a smile a mile wide. This nigga was too happy, so I already knew that his ass got some pussy.

"Tell your brother to leave me alone then," she told him, giving him a hug.

"Not too tight. You know a nigga still broke," he joked.

"I'm sorry." She apologized.

"It's cool. Y'all come in," he said, moving to the side behind Em.

I watched as he wrapped her into his arms from behind and kissed her hair. She blushed, and I could see the happiness dance in both of their eyes. I was happy because my brother deserved a chick that was for him, and that dirty ass Siya wasn't it. But I was also confused because last time I checked, she lived here, and they were living happily ever after.

"Babe, take Zoie in the kitchen to get some of the breakfast you cooked. I'ma holla at my lil' brother for a second then we'll come in there to join y'all," he told her.

Turning around, she nodded her head and stood on her tiptoes. He gave her a quick peck on the lips. Zoie and I exchanged looks as we watched the two of them interact. She had a smirk on her face, and I was just in shock. I never once saw Myeke affectionate with Siya for as long as they were together, and he didn't ever call her babe. He called her ass by her name, so to see him caking with Em was different, but a good different nonetheless.

"Okay. Come on, Zoie," Emily said, walking in the direction of the kitchen.

"You gon' be okay by yourself?" Zoie turned and asked me.

"Yeah, I'll be fine, mama. Just go fix my plate, and I'll be in there in a minute," I reassured her.

"Okay." She nodded.

When she turned to walk away, I smacked her on the ass just to watch it jiggle. Turning around blushing, she shot me a bird, and I gave her a wink. We both stood in silence just watching them walk away.

"When that happen?" I asked him when they disappeared.

"A couple weeks ago," he replied. "C'mon," he said, walking off towards his office.

When we got inside, I took a seat in one of the chairs in front of his desk and waited while he moved around in the closet looking for something. Two minutes later, he came back in the room with a kilo in his hands. Tossing it towards me, I caught it and looked at it. It had the same blue packaging as the ones I took from Sac's punk ass.

"You know what that is, B?" he asked, sitting on the edge of his desk.

"Do I look like I'm retarded, my nigga. It's a kilo of cocaine," I replied, rolling my eyes.

"Not just any cocaine. It's pure Colombian coke. It's the shit that Rod was getting and the shit Pops was getting before him. That's the same shit that I flood the streets wit'. The shit that I found in your closet," he replied.

"That's the shit I got from Sac after I blew his brains out. I never knew it was yours. I've never seen your coke, and this definitely don't look like the shit that I'm used to gettin' from him. But then again, I'on serve the shit. I just mule it. Collect my bread and dip," I told him honestly.

Setting the brick back on the desk, I looked at him for the first time and watched the vein in his head pop out. I knew that he was in his feelings about how nonchalant I was about my dealings with Deuce. I tried to tell him the shit in a sweet way, but he wasn't trying to hear it. He wanted to pop shit, so I was gon' give it to his ass straight, no chaser. That's what he wanted, so that's what he was getting.

"The reason you never seen that shit from me because we never wanted this shit for you. Before Pops got knocked, he begged me not to get in it, but I was hardheaded... always following Rod, and when Rod put me on, he made me promise not to do the same wit' you. When he died, I vowed to keep my promise, and I been doin' that shit."

"That's the thing though, Key. I'm grown. Can't nobody make decisions for me. I can't live off your handouts for the rest of my life. You made the shit perfectly clear that, that's how I been eating by all the shit you threw in my face at the hospital. I wasn't feeling that shit. That's why I been making my own way," I explained.

Running his hand down his face, he sighed before looking at me.

"Look, about that shit. I shouldn't have said that shit. A nigga was pissed off, but I shouldn't have let that shit fly out my mouth."

"Say less. I already forgave you."

Nodding his head, he stroked his goatee like he was thinking about something.

"I ain't tryin' to change the subject, but what's goin' on wit' you and that doctor chick, and where Siya's crazy ass? I know she ain't just sitting upstairs while you parade another chick around the crib," I asked.

"Damn, I forgot you don't know. Shit been mad crazy, and I been trying to damn near forget about the shit that happened," he said, shaking his head. "Siya set me up to get wet up. I'on know how she know that nigga, but she do."

"Dead ass?"

"Dead ass, my nigga. When I get my hands on that bitch, I'ma fuck her ass up. I just can't find her. Brooklyn only so big, and the bitch ain't got no friends. I'on know where the fuck she could have gone," he said, stressed.

"What exactly do you know about her?" I questioned.

"What the fuck that's supposed to mean, son?"

"Calm down, Key, damn. You always ready to go the fuck off over simple shit. You buggin', my nigga. Just think about it, tho'. What do you know about Siya, for real? You been wit' lil' mama what, eight years? You've never met her family. You probably seen her moms once, and she supposed to be from Philly," I told him.

I could tell that he was thinking about what I said because that ugly ass vein in his forehead started to throb fast as hell.

"That's fuckin' crazy. I ain't never thought about that shit. She could be living a whole double life, and a nigga wouldn't even know shit."

"You gotta find that bitch and quick. She knows too much shit about you, and you don't know shit about her. I wouldn't be surprised if that bitch set you up so that she could rob you," I told him, shaking my head.

When he didn't say shit, I knew I was close, if not completely right. I always felt like something was grimy about her ass, but I ain't think that she was that fucking dirty. Hell, he was the father of her son for crying out loud.

"She thought she robbed a nigga. She got me for about seventy grand or so," he admitted, shrugging his shoulders.

"Seventy grand! You don't seem too broke up about the shit. That's hella money, B."

"Yeah, but she can have that shit. She ain't get half of what a nigga worth. C'mon," he said, standing back up and picking back up the kilo off the desk.

He started walking back towards the closet, and I stood up, looking at that nigga like he was losing his mind.

"Nigga, I'on know what type of fuck shit you on, but I ain't goin' in that lil' ass closet wit' yo' ass," I told him.

"Shut the hell up before I smack yo' ass," he said, laughing. "Bring yo' homophobic ass on and quit runnin' ya pussy lickers so much. You actually might learn somethin', son."

"Yeah, aight," I replied, following behind him.

Stepping inside the walk-in closet, he closed the door behind us before moving some clothes out of the way and exposing a crack in the wall. Hitting a switch, a blue keypad popped up on the wall that wasn't there before, and the wall opened up when he entered the numbers.

Pushing the door open, he stepped inside, and I walked in behind him, curious as hell. My eyes got wide as saucers as I looked at all the money that lined the walls and the few keys of cocaine that sat on a shelf. Returning the kilo he had in his hands, he turned towards me to gauge my reaction.

"This you?" I asked, picking up a stack of hundreds and flipping through it.

"Everything except about a hundred grand. It was Rod's that he had set aside for your twenty-first birthday," he admitted, and my eyes doubled in size.

"A hundred k? Bro, you lying?"

"I'm dead ass. But wit' the way shit been goin' on, I'ma go ahead and give it to you along wit' the fifty I had put up for you."

"I can't take that shit, man. It wouldn't feel right," I told him, shaking my head.

A hundred and fifty thousand was a sweet ass lick, but I wasn't the one that worked for it. I could say it was a gift, but what the fuck was I gon' do with that type of money, living in the fucking projects?

"You can, and you will. Just tell a nigga that you gon' leave all them dope boy ambitions alone, and let me handle this side of it. You'll never want for anything as long as I got air in my lungs, but I understand what you meant by wanting to stand on your own two, so I got a proposition for you," he said.

"And what's that?"

"I been puttin' in the money to go legit. I'm opening up a strip club out in Jersey and one out in Philly. You can manage them for me. You make your own money and, in a way, you your own boss. You'll run both. I'll just own the buildings."

"Nigga, did you forget that I'm not legal?"

"But you will be twenty next month, so it's only right," he said, shrugging his shoulders.

Thinking over what he said, I finally agreed, and the thought of having my own money sounded better and better. We sat in the office for a few more minutes, chopping it up and putting together a game plan to get at Siya, Deuce, and them niggas that violated Zoie.

The dope game wasn't meant for me, and I was willing to leave all this street shit alone but, for now, I had to not only help my brother tie up his loose ends but do the same with mine as well. Walking back in the kitchen, we sat around eating, laughing, and joking with the girls, and I was just happy to see Zoie smiling and having a good time.

I would do anything to keep a smile on her face, and that's how I knew I made the right decision for what I was about to do. I just hoped she said yes.

CHAPTER TWELVE

Zoie

I didn't expect for us to spend the entire day over at Myeke's with him and Emily, but I was glad that we did. It was fun, and it felt good to see O'Hajee smiling again. Looking out the window, I started to think about everything that had happened between us.

We hadn't been together long, but it seemed as if the world didn't want us together. I never thought for a second that I would be with O'Hajee. He was arrogant, flashy, and his mouth would make you want to punch him directly in it without so much of a second thought. But he was my happiness. Being with him was my safe haven.

I could be pissed at him about the situation with Monica and the stuff with my mom, but he had already broken things off with me at the time, and my mom was a grown ass woman. O'Hajee didn't make her smoke that shit. That was a decision that she made all on her own.

When I realized that we took the Manhattan exit, I finally broke out of my daydream and looked over at O'Hajee.

"Where are we goin'?" I asked, sitting up in the seat.

"Just ride, lil' nigga. Let me handle this," he said, glancing over toward me and winking.

"Boy, don't play wit' me," I warned.

"Just sit back and chill. Let me handle this. You takin' all the fun out of this shit," he told me, rolling his eyes.

"I told you about doin' that, babe. You look like a girl." I laughed, and he shot me an evil glare.

I couldn't do anything but laugh harder. He couldn't be mad at me for telling the truth. I felt any man that rolled his eyes looked that way. O'Hajee was all man, and anyone with eyes could see that.

"Fuck it, son. We goin' back home. Ain't nobody got time for your shit talkin'," he said, preparing to make a U-turn.

"Okay, okay, I'm sorry. You don't look entirely like a female," I teased.

"Zoie!"

"I'm sorry." I apologized through giggles. "You just make it so easy. Isn't that what you tell me?"

"But that's different."

"How?"

He didn't respond because he knew that what he said was dumb. Men could always dish out dumb shit but couldn't take it.

"Aww. I'm sorry. Are you mad at me?" I asked, reaching over and pinching his cheek.

"Bro. If you don't gon' wit' that shit, I'll take ya spoiled ass home for real," he said.

"Ugh, you're no fun." I huffed as I sat back in the seat and crossed my arms over my chest.

"Cry baby."

Ignoring him, I sent a text to River. I hadn't seen her much since I started spending time with Hajee, and now that I was home from my stay at the hospital, it was about time that we hung out. I missed her.

Me: Where's my River?

River: Where you left her. *eye roll emoji*

Me: Don't be like that sugar. You know I love you. *smiley face*

River: Yeah yeah. Tell me anything. Wyd?

Me: Being held captive in a car by O'Hajee. He won't tell me where we're going and I'm about to punch him.

River: Lol girl please. You know damn well you ain't punch that man.

Me: Like dead ass sis. He mad annoying. All I want to know is where we going and he ignoring me like a female. Fuckin' crybaby.

River: Look who's talking. Bih, you better let that man take you away. Just throw that shit in a circle and get pampered.

Me: Ughh bye! You aren't helping.

River: SUCK HIS DICK BITCH! Okay bye. I love you too! I will be there to see you tomorrow!

Me: Never said I loved you whore.

River: But you do slut so bye. Get enough dick for the both of us. Issa drought for your girl. I'm practicing abstinence.

Me: We both know that's a lie lol

River: Lmao ikr but it sounded good.

"You gon' keep textin' on your phone, or you gon' get out the car?" O'Hajee asked.

I hadn't even noticed the car came to a stop, since I was laughing at River's dumb self. She was a little rough around the edges, but that was my bih all day. Looking up, I realized we were in front of a brownstone. There was a porch light on, and a few other lights seemed to be on inside.

"Who lives here?" I asked, unsnapping my seat belt.

"Son, get ya ass out the car. It's brick as fuck out here, and I ain't got no jacket on," he complained, closing the driver's door.

Rolling my eyes up into my head, I got out the car and closed the door behind me. I didn't even acknowledge his comment about it being cold. The summer was turning into fall fast, but it was decent outside. O'Hajee's ass just needed thicker blood. He was always cold.

Grabbing ahold of my hand, he pulled me up the driveway and pulled out a set of keys. Opening the door, he waited for me to enter before he walked in and closed the door behind him. Stepping further inside the apartment, I realized that it was mainly empty. There were a few pieces of furniture here and there, but nothing too major.

"You like it?" he asked, walking up behind me and wrapping his arms around my waist.

"I mean, it's nice for someone who doesn't have kids. I mean, they don't seem to have too much of anything," I replied. "Wait, Hajee.

Which one of your boy's bachelor pads you got me in?"

"That's because you haven't decorated it yet."

"Wait. Do you mean...?" I asked, turning around in his arms.

"Yeah. It was my brother Rod's. He never stayed here though. Something about the hood kept him comin' back. Myeke told me I could move here wit' Moms, but she ain't want it, and he got his own crib. So, I thought that we could move in here. I mean, that's if you want to," he said, looking down into my eyes.

"Of course I do. I used to always want to stay in a brownstone after watching *The Cosby Show* as a kid." I squealed, kissing him on the jaw and running around.

There were two bedrooms and two baths. It wasn't huge, but it was a nice size for just the two of us. The kitchen was cute as hell, and I could see myself in there plenty of days. I could tell that being here reminded him of his brother, but it meant a lot to me that he would want to get me away from Pink Houses, no matter how much it bothered him.

"Baby, I love it," I told him, taking a seat next to him on the only couch in the living room. "Thank you."

"Say less. You ain't gotta thank me. This for both of us, and I meant what I said, Zoie. Nothing and nobody else will hurt you while there's air in my lungs. I failed you once. I can't see myself doin' it again," he admitted, rubbing my cheek.

"I love you."

"I love you more, mamas," he replied, kissing me on the lips.

We kissed for a few minutes before I felt him harden against my butt, and I unintentionally tensed up. He must've sensed it because he broke the kiss and placed one on my forehead.

"I'm sorry," I told him.

"Don't be. You been through a lot of shit, ma, and I'll never make you do something that you ain't ready to do yet. C'mon, let's get outta here. A nigga hungry, and I know Moms waiting up on us."

"Okay," I replied standing up.

After he locked up, we got back in the car and headed back to the one place that neither of us wanted to be, but now that I knew I had a place I could call my own, being here made it a little easier. Things were finally getting back on track, but I couldn't help feeling that this was all temporary. Praying that I was just paranoid, I sat back and enjoyed the ride home.

CHAPTER THIRTEEN

Siya

A month later.

$\mathcal{I}$ was gripping the steering wheel so tight that my knuckles started to turn white. I sat in my car watching Myeke kiss some woman in a suit, on the lips, before she got in her car and left. I don't know what possessed me to come back to New York, but here I was, and the fact that this nigga had another bitch living in the house we shared had me tight.

Granted, I tried to get him killed, but damn. Let my side of the bed get cold before you bring a new bitch in it. When her car passed me, I waited thirty seconds or so before pulling out behind her and following her. It seemed like I followed her forever before she pulled into University Hospital in Brooklyn.

"Oh, you done got you an ol' educated bitch, huh, Myeke?" I asked out loud.

Finding a parking spot, I got out of the car and followed behind her, curious as to what it was about her. I mean, I could be honest and say that she was gorgeous. The color of her skin reminded me of copper, and she looked young. Older than me, but young nonetheless.

Pulling the black hoodie over my head, I pulled it tight, scared that someone might notice me stalking this lady. She was walking around all smiles without a care in the world, and I would bet my last dollar that dick was the cause of it. Myeke's dick. My dick.

"Dr. James!" I heard someone call out.

Hearing the feet run in our direction, I thought I was caught, but the person just sped past me. Hearing her name be called, she turned around on her heels with a smile plastered on her face.

Doctor, huh? I thought, taking a seat and picking up a magazine, pretending to be interested in it.

"Hey, Bryan. What's up?" she greeted.

"Hey, Emily. I know this is so unprofessional of me, but I was wondering if you could cancel my appointment with Mr. Compton this week?" he asked her.

Looking around to make sure no one was looking at them, she looked back at him and pulled him to the side, a little closer to where I was sitting.

"You know you can't be saying stuff like that out loud," she reminded him.

"Why, because you're banging your ex patient? Girl, please. As fine as he is, if he were gay, I'd fuck him too," he told her, laughing.

"Oh gosh. Kill the visual." She laughed. "But sure, I don't mind.

I'm sure he'll love to get out of therapy with you. Or as he calls it, torture."

"Please. All that man, and he sensitive to a little pulling and tugging."

"I don't think it's the pulling and tugging that he's sensitive about. It may be the fact that you have a habit of hitting him on the butt when he's done, like you two are playing basketball."

"I mean, everyone needs a little encouragement and reassurance that they're doing a good job." He laughed.

"I can't with you. How long will you be gone?" she asked him, changing the subject, and I was glad she did because I didn't want to think about anyone touching my man. Male or female.

"I don't know, girl. Richard called me and said that I better be packed when he gets in tonight, and if I wasn't, he was leaving me here. I have a little vacation time saved up and no active patients other than your boo thang, so I said, why not. I feel pretty good that he can manage without me, especially with the good doctor on his side," he joked.

"Bye, Bryan. I have to head to my office and read over this patient's file, but I'll be sure to tell him what you said."

"Thanks, boo! I'll text you later."

"Okay."

Shaking her head at him, she started back on her walk, and I started back on my hunt for answers. I originally didn't plan to make my presence known to her or anyone else, but hearing that things were kind of serious between her and Myeke, I knew I needed to step to this tramp and let her know that I was back to take claim to my man.

I worked too hard to be with him to let some bitch swoop in and take it away. We would never be together again, but I could make sure that he was never with another bitch again after me.

"Um, excuse me," I called out just as she reached an office door.

"Yes, can I help you?" she asked before turning around and seeing me.

Pulling the hood off my head, I gave her the once over and got even more pissed off that she was prettier up close. I just wanted to carve her pretty little flawless skin up. Wonder if Myeke will still want her, if her ass was walking around here looking like Joker off *Batman?*

"So, you're Myeke's flavor of the month."

"Excuse me?" she asked, looking around to make sure no one was around.

"Myeke Compton. I mean, you are fucking him, right?" I asked.

"What I do and who I do it with, is not really any of your concern. Now if you would please leave, I have things that I have to do," she replied, spinning on her heels, dismissing me.

Grabbing ahold of her arm, I spun her around so that she was facing me, before closing the small distance between us and lowering my voice.

"Listen, bitch. Stay the fuck away from him or I will make your life a living hell. Myeke is my man, and I'd be damned if I let some white lab coat wearing bitch swoop in and take something that belongs to me." I was seething.

I half expected her to be scared by my threat, but this crazy bitch laughed. I don't mean no little giggle either. I mean a full-blown, hold your stomach laugh. When she got her laughing under control, she closed the rest of the space between us, and she was standing so close that I could smell the coffee and blueberry muffin that she had for breakfast, on her breath.

"No, you listen. If he was truly your man, you wouldn't be here tryin' to throw your weight around. You would be checking him, not me. And move around with your lil' ass threats because this 'white lab coat wearing bitch' as you called me, can whoop your ass and make you disappear without so much of a trace. I don't take too kindly to threats.

Just because I don't live in the hood like a gutta rat such as yourself, doesn't mean I forgot where the fuck I came from. I was born and raised in Brevoort Houses, boo. Don't let me being nice fool you. Now as I said, get the fuck on. I got shit to do," she said, spinning around and walking into her office before slamming the door in my face.

I had to admit to myself that miss goody two shoes had me a little shook. She was still proper as hell, but I could see it in her eyes that everything she said, she meant. Instead of knocking on her door, I pulled my hood back on and made a beeline towards the exit, and bumped into someone as I rounded the corner.

"Damn, my bad, ma," he said when he knocked me over. "Let me help you up."

"NO! I got it!" I yelled, jumping up and speed walking away.

I could feel his eyes on me, and it took all my willpower not to run all the way back to my car. What were the chances that I would be following his bitch and he would just show up and bump into me? I had been hearing Myeke's voice for so long that I was positive I would recognize it through ten brick walls and a thunderstorm.

I didn't release the breath I was holding until I was safely back in my car and pulled out of the hospital parking lot. That was close, and I wasn't ready for him to see me yet, especially since I didn't have Karson with me as leverage. He was out at my aunt's house where I was staying while I was still here. But soon enough, I would make my presence known, and when I did, he would have no choice but to give me his undivided attention.

I was playing with fire, but when it was all said and done, either Myeke would be with me, or I would start killing everyone he loved one by one. Starting with that uppity bitch he was laying pipe to.

CHAPTER FOURTEEN

Myeke

$\mathcal{I}$ watched the lady I knocked down for a few seconds before shaking my head. I was a menacing looking nigga, but damn. Women didn't normally run away from me. They ran to my ass, even when I didn't want them to. It wasn't only that she was wearing a hoodie pulled tight over her face; it was something about her presence that stuck out to me, but I couldn't put my finger on it.

Pushing the thoughts to the back of my head, I knocked on Em's office door and walked in when she said it was open.

"Damn, ma. You good? You look like you ready to go a few rounds wit' Tyson," I joked.

She looked mad as hell, and the evil glare she was giving me didn't go unnoticed. I wasn't sure what I did in the hour and a half that I didn't see her, but it wasn't good. Lil' mama looked like she wanted to chop a nigga's dick off and feed it to a dog.

"Why you lookin' at me like that? What, someone cut you off on the interstate or some shit?"

"No, better. One of your lil' bitches decided to come pay me a visit up here. She wanted me to stay away from 'her man,'" she said, using air quotes. "This is my fuckin' job, Myeke. I can't have your lil' hood rats coming up here whenever the fuck they feel like it. I could lose my job for fuckin' one of their asses up, and if I lose my job, you better believe, I'm fuckin' your pretty ass up right after." She seethed as she pointed her finger at me.

"You think I'm pretty?" I asked, breaking out into a wide smile.

"Key! This is serious!" she yelled, hitting me in the chest.

"Whoa!" I said, grabbing her hand and pulling her toward me. "First, calm the hell down. I can see you mad, but quit yellin' at me because I'm not yellin' at yo' lil' ass. And second, don't put ya hands on me. I understand you upset, but I'm liable to smack ya ass back. I don't hit women, but my mama always told me that when someone hit me, hit they ass back."

"Well, I wouldn't have to hit you if you knew how to control your bitches," she sassed.

If I wasn't so confused, I would be turned the hell on. Seeing Em boss up on me had me ready to pull down her slacks and bend her ass over this desk until I fucked her attitude away. Shit, it was still possible.

"I don't talk in riddles, ma, and I damn sure ain't got no bitches. You the only one getting this big motherfucka put in yo' life. I'm good fucking one bitch," I told her, causing her to hit me again.

"Aye, what I say about your hands, Em. I may not hit you, but I'll fuck the shit out of you," I warned.

"Watch your mouth then."

Huffing, she walked around her desk and took a seat in the chair before running her hands through her hair. Locking the door behind me, I made my way around the back of her desk before pulling her up to stand in front of me.

"I'm sorry, ma. I really don't know who came up here but they lying. They trying to take you out yo' element. I ain't fuckin' with no other girls. I got what I want right here," I explained.

"Tell me anything," she replied, rolling her eyes.

"What you don't believe me now? Have I ever lied to you?"

"No. Not that I know of."

"Well then. I'm sorry that someone fucked up your day because of me. Let me make it up to you," I told her, unbuttoning her slacks and letting them slide off her hips.

"What are you doing?" she asked but didn't attempt to stop me.

"Step out of these."

Doing as she was told, she stepped out of them and kicked her pants to the side. Turning her around to face her desk, I bit my lip, getting an eye full of her round ass in the red thong she had on. I was glad that I wore a pair of joggers up here as I undid the drawstring and pulled them down to my knees.

Bending her over her desk, I pushed her thong to the side and rubbed the head of my dick up and down her slit before smirking at how wet she was. Pushing my way inside her, I gave her a second to adjust before I started to give her long deep strokes.

"Ssss. Key, I haveee. Ooouuu. I haveee surgery in an hour," she moaned out in a whisper.

"Sssss, ma. Move ya hand," I said through gritted teeth. "That gives me thirty minutes. Let zaddy take care of you."

"Okayyyyy," she cried out.

I was trying not to fuck the shit out of her because people were more than likely walking by her office door, but the way she was moaning out, I'm sure someone already knew what was going on behind this door. Looking around her desk, I was trying to find something I could put in her mouth to keep her quiet. Coming up empty handed, I settled with a piece of computer paper.

Balling it up in my hand, I shoved it in her mouth just as she started moaning to muffle the sound.

"Bite down on that shit," I groaned.

"Mmmmmm."

Laying her flat across the desk, I grabbed ahold to her waist and picked up my pace. The only thing that could be heard in the room were groans, skin slapping, and her muffled moans. Feeling her pussy start to spit on my dick with each stroke, I reached around her and pinched her clit just as her walls started to constrict.

Feeling myself about to nut, I threw my head back and started fucking her faster until I felt the semen shoot out the head of my dick.

"Argghhh! Fuckkkk, girl!" I moaned out, forgetting where we were for two seconds.

It took me a second to catch my breath as I eased out of her and smacked her on the booty. Still lying flat on her desk, I stepped to the side, watching my baby try to catch her breath. I wanted to laugh so bad as I watched her spit out the ball of paper I shoved in her mouth and try to lick her tongue out to make her mouth moist again.

"Really, Key? Paper?" she asked, standing to her feet.

"Shit, you was loud, and that was the only thing I could think of," I told her, shrugging my shoulders.

"Hand me my purse, please, so we can get cleaned up before someone decides to knock on my door."

Doing as she asked, she dug in the purse and pulled out a set of baby wipes and cleaned me off before handling herself. No words were passed between us as we adjusted our clothes, but just seeing her move that thong back in place had me ready to say fuck her surgery and fuck what I had to do after this, just so I could slide back between them cheeks.

"What are you doin' up here anyway?" she asked, pulling her clothes back on, checking herself in the mirror on her wall.

"Oh damn, I almost forgot. You left your phone at the crib," I told her, reaching in my pocket and handing it to her.

"Thank God you found it. I wouldn't know what to do if I had to work a whole shift without it," she said, taking the phone out of my hand and checking her messages.

"Better not nobody be callin' or textin' yo' ass while you at work, but me and ya mama."

"Why? Is my baby jealous?" she asked, smiling.

"Nah. Never that, ma. To be jealous, that means I would have to be an insecure ass nigga, and that ain't me. I just know what's mine, and don't nobody need to be texting my girl," I replied honestly.

"Well, I'on think my other niggas know that."

"Get fucked up, youngin."

Grabbing her up into my arms, I wrapped her up in my arms and palmed her ass while looking down into her eyes. Everything about this girl was breathtaking, and she had a nigga sprung something serious. I was with Siya for damn near eight years, and she never made me feel the way that I feel whenever I was in Emily's presence.

"Why are you looking at me like that?" she questioned, breaking me out of my thoughts.

"You mad beautiful, ma. You know that?"

"I think this man I know has told me once or twice," she commented and started giggling when I pinched her on her butt. "I'm just jokin', baby, sheesh. But thank you. You don't look half bad yourself," she told me, smiling.

"Say less," I replied, kissing her on the forehead and then the lips. "Let me get outta here though. I need to go link up wit' my boy Al and check on a few things."

"Okay, baby. See you tonight."

"Fa sho. You stayin' at the crib again tonight?"

"I'm over there so much, Key, I don't remember what the inside of my house looks like."

"Bro, you draggin' it." I laughed. "If you don't want to spend time wit' a nigga, ma, just say that. I can give you ya space."

It would be hard as hell to give her space, but if that's what she needed, then I would do it. Well, I'd at least attempt to. Couldn't make any promises.

"Boy, hush. You know that's not it. I'm goin' to go by and grab some clothes for the week and then I'll head that way after work. Want me to cook, or you want to order in?"

"I'll cook. You just tell me what time you pullin' up and I got you," I said.

"Sounds good to me. Now that someone has knocked out thirty minutes of my prep time, I need to rush through these notes and go check on my patient before I have to do this surgery," she informed me.

"Let me get out your way then, and be good, mini Laila Ali," I joked, kissing her on the forehead.

"I'll try. Just keep your females away from me," she said, reaching up for a kiss on the lips.

"Yeah, aight."

Finally letting her go, I kissed her lips again before getting ready to leave the room.

"What did she look like? The broad that came up here, I mean," I asked, because I realized I never asked.

"Um, maybe a little lighter than me. Black hair. Kinda slim. Real ghetto. Sound like she from out of Philly somewhere," she answered, shrugging her shoulders while looking through her notes.

Nah, it can't be. She ain't that fuckin' stupid, I thought.

"This chick... did she have a lip ring and a beauty mark in the

143

corner of her eye?" I asked.

"Yeah. How'd you know that?" she questioned, finally looking at me.

"Nothing, baby. Let me handle it. Call me on your lunch break," I said over my shoulder and left the room before she had a chance to respond.

She was gon' have a million and two questions later, but for now, I had to get to where Al was. Siya was a lot dumber than I thought. I'd been searching high and low for shorty for over two months now, and when she finally decides to resurface, it's at my girl's job. If I knew her as well as I believe I do, she wasn't gon' leave East New York just yet. She was going to stick around and try to make shit go left with me and Emily, and when she decided to make her move, I would be waiting on her ass.

* * *

Pulling up to the Pink Houses, I hopped out my truck and saw Al's car across the way. I was glad he beat me here so I wouldn't have to wait on him. Nodding my head at the people that were posted up outside, I kept on my way. It was plenty of bitches outside trying to get my attention, but they were used to me ignoring them by now. I had always been a one-woman man, and that shit would never change.

Putting my key in the door, I could hear voices coming from the other side, and I already knew what was going on. Opening the door, I was greeted by my moms, Hajee, Zoie, and Al sitting in the living room, joking around at something my moms was saying.

"Yo, Moms, don't nobody wanna hear that shit, B!" Hajee faked

PORSCHEA JADE

shuddered like he was disgusted.

"Make me come over there and fuck you up about that damn mouth," she warned. "But hell, me and yo' daddy did used to go at it. I know you ain't talkin' by the way you be tryin' to kill that poor girl in the next room. Sex is natural, and if I wasn't fuckin' ya daddy on the regular, none of y'all asses would be here, so shut up," she told him.

You know that moment when you know you walked in on the wrong part of the conversation? Yep, that was me right now.

"Moms!" Zoie gasped, embarrassed.

"My bad, baby, but I had to prove a point. The way that mouth be runnin', he be makin' me wish I swallowed his lil' ass wit' the other kids that I should've had. I must've swallowed the wrong one and had his ass instead."

"Yo, bro! Ew, Moms. This the type of stuff you on when I'm not around?" I asked with a play grimace on my face.

"Hey, baby! Don't start your shit. All I was sayin' was how me and your father was back in the day because Zoie reminds me of myself. She needs to get a little better at smacking this fool in the mouth, but she puts him in his place when he need it. He the one started talkin' smack. I had to pull his cards since he wanted to pull mine," she told me, walking over to give me a hug.

Pulling away from me, she gave me the stank face, and I looked down at her confused.

"Damn. What I do now?" I questioned.

"What woman you been up under because it ain't that bird brain

145

bitch you call ya baby mama, and you smiling a lil' too much for it to be that hoe. Who is she?" my mom asked.

Breaking out in a smile, I thought about Em, and at first, I was a little scared to bring her around my mom because she was so soft, and I didn't want my mom to scare her off. But the way she bossed up on me at the hospital and let that gutta side out of her, I knew she would fit right in, and my mom would love her.

"Her name is Emily. She's a surgeon over at University Hospital-Brooklyn." I smiled.

"I gotta meet this girl. You didn't even correct me for talkin' about that tramp. She gotta be special if she pulled them claws out of you."

Shrugging my shoulders, I still didn't correct her about Siya because it wasn't my place no more. She was everything my moms was saying and then some. My only concern was hunting the bitch down so that I could get to my son. Then I was killing that bitch without any other thoughts. She wanted to play wit' my son, and I was going to show her why the fuck I was the nigga I was in the streets.

"Looks like I ain't the only one gettin' it," Hajee commented.

"Shut yo' ass up. I see why moms be wantin' to go in ya mouth, nigga," I told him.

"Moms, you gon' like Em tho'. She ain't nothin' like Siya," Hajee told her.

"He done met her too? Wait, pause... Is this the same doctor from the hospital? Your doctor?" she asked, finally catching on.

"Moms, I was startin' to think you was a lil' slow," Hajee joked.

"But yeah, that's her."

"How long has this been going on?"

"Since the day I left the hospital," I replied, avoiding eye contact.

"I should've known ya sneaky ass was on something when you told me I didn't have to come see you every day. I want her at dinner next week," she told me, pointing her finger at me.

"Mama Tina, can I come?" Al asked, finally speaking up.

"This nigga." I laughed.

"Everybody can come. Bring whoever it is y'all fuckin', and I'ma do the same," she said, causing all of us to stop laughing.

The mugs that Hajee, Al, and I had on our faces made Zoie clear her throat. When the fuck did my mom start seeing someone? Let alone, long enough to feel that nigga was good enough to meet us. I was a grown ass man, and I still wasn't feeling the idea.

Call it what you want, but I was sensitive about my moms and little brother. They were all I had, and I didn't like anyone getting close to them without me knowing about it. Zoie was the exception, but I've known that Hajee was in love with her since she was thirteen. She just wasn't hip until now.

"Pops know about this?" I asked, mugging her.

"Don't question me. I'm grown, and if you must know, it was your father's idea. He's not in denial. He knows that he's never getting out. He doesn't want me to be lonely for the rest of my life," she replied.

I could see my pops telling her that, but shit, she wouldn't be lonely. She had us, hell.

"You don't need no man; you got us," I told her.

"Boy, please. Hajee done moved out to Manhattan wit' Zoie. You live all the way out in Syosset, and Al fuck more bitches than he can keep count of to come check on me. I'm not gettin' any younger, and this isn't up for debate. I'm bringin' him to meet you guys next weekend, and you will be on your best behavior. Do you understand me?" she asked, looking around at the three of us.

It got so quiet that you could hear a pin drop. Al acted like he was busy on his phone. O'Hajee's arms were folded across his chest, mumbling to himself like the was a kid. If this was any other time, I would've laughed at his spoiled ass. And I was looking down like I ain't hear shit she said.

"Do I make myself clear?" she asked again, raising her voice a little this time.

"Yeah, aight," I mumbled, followed by grumbling from Hajee and Al.

"Good. Now, Zoie, come help me in the kitchen. I'm sure the boys have somethin' to talk about since they're all in my living room at the same time."

"Yes, ma'am," Zoie told her before reaching over and kissing O'Hajee and following our mom in the living room.

"And I'm not a boy!" Hajee shouted.

"Hajee, shut the hell up! Yep, I definitely should have swallowed you!" she yelled back.

The look on his face was priceless. Al and I looked at each other before laughing hard as hell. That little nigga was tight as hell. He knew she was just joking, but that shit still hurt his feelings.

"C'mon, let's go in the back. I'on need Moms hearin' what I'm about to tell y'all," I told them before heading in the back toward my old bedroom.

After they took seats on my bed, I closed the door and leaned against the dresser before I started talking.

"Siya's back. She went to the hospital and tried to spook Em," I told them.

"Sis alright?" Al asked.

"Shit, she better than alright. I didn't see what happened, but when I saw her, she looked like she was ready to lay Siya flat on her back. My lil' mama even bossed up on me," I said smiling, thinking about how cute she was when mad. "That's not even the worst part though."

"What is it then?" Hajee asked, leaning forward, resting his elbows on his knees.

"I'm about 100 percent positive that she ran into me, leaving Em's office."

"And you didn't snatch the bitch up?" Al asked.

"I didn't know it was her. She had this hoodie on, pulled tight over her face. She ran into me coming around the corner, and fell down. I offered to help her out, and she yelled 'no' before speed walking out of the hospital. I thought the shit was a lil' odd, but I didn't think nothing of it until I asked Em what the woman looked like that stepped to her.

She described Siya," I explained.

"She must got a death wish," Al commented.

"Facts. Shorty bold as fuck," Hajee added, nodding his head.

"I can't do shit but agree wit' you, but since she was long gone by the time Em told me who she was, I have no idea what she was driving and where she would go. I done had someone sitting on her mom's house since I woke up, and she ain't been there."

"She ain't that stupid. She wouldn't go back there knowin' the shit that you know she did," Hajee said. "She gotta have someone, though, that would know where she at," he pointed out, whispering more to himself than to me.

The room fell silent as we started to think. It seemed like at the same time, all three of our heads popped up.

"Monica!"

"Bro, Zoie ain't gon' be feeling this shit at all! She gon' snap out on my ass," Hajee said, running his hand through his hair.

"You the only connection between the two. If she can at least give us something, you won't have to play her too close. Just fuck wit' her enough to get the information we need," I told him.

"I know what I gotta do. You just gotta explain that shit to that crazy ass girl in there. Ever since she forgave a nigga, she ain't been playin' no types of games when it came to me, at all. Let Monica name flash across my screen in front of her. She go to asking questions like 'Are you bleeding?' 'Is the baby okay?' 'You got a doctor's appointment?' I be wanting to laugh, but after getting smacked the first two times, I just let her have that shit."

"Lil' sis got yo' ass trained." Al laughed.

Hajee shot his ass a bird, but he couldn't do shit but laugh too, because he already knew what it was. Zoie changed my little brother, but it was for the best, so I wasn't complaining one bit.

Getting off the dresser, I opened the room door and stuck my head out.

"Lil' sis! Come here for a second!" I yelled into the hallway.

"My nigga, do you want me to die!" Hajee whispered.

"Shut yo' scary ass up. It's now or never, but we gotta do this," I told him, taking my seat back on my dresser.

A few seconds later, Zoie came down the hallway and leaned against the doorframe.

"What's up, Key?" she asked.

"Step in here real quick. I need to run some shit by you," I told her.

Stepping in the room, she closed the door behind her and cut her eyes at O'Hajee, who was avoiding eye contact with her. He looked guilty as hell, and she had her eyebrow raised like she was two seconds away from going to jack his ass up.

"What did you do?" she asked him, folding her arms across her chest.

"Damn, lil' nigga. Why you automatically assume I did some shit?" he asked, feigning hurt.

"It could be the fact that you look guilty as hell, or the fact that you avoidin' lookin' at me. Pick one. Hajee, I swear if ya ass is on that bullshit, I'ma smack the shit out ya punk ass."

"Damn, it's like that?"

"You shouldn't even have to ask," she shot back.

"Yeah, aight. We'll see. Keep that same energy for when we get home and I fold ya ass in a full nelson," he told her, and her face flushed red.

These freaks, I thought, smirking.

"Calm down, lil' sis. He ain't on no foul shit. I'd smack that nigga for you if he was," I reassured her. "I do need Hajee to do something for me," I admitted.

"If it's the drug shit, the answer is no, Myeke. He already got one body. He don't need another one," she said, shaking her head.

Shooting a look over at Hajee, he just shrugged his shoulders. I respected the fact that he told her, but damn.

"It's not that. I need him to help me find my baby mama," I told her.

"Okay. How do you expect him to do that if you can't find her?"

"Did Hajee tell you everything about me gettin' shot?" I decided to ask so that she understood how serious this shit was.

"No," she answered, shaking her head. "He told me it wasn't his business to tell. Only thing he said was that it was street shit."

"I appreciate it, but I wish he would've. My baby mama set me up to get wet up," I confessed.

The anger that flashed over her face was instant. Her face turned red, and her eyebrows dipped at the news.

"Bro! Where that bum ass bitch at! You don't even need Hajee. He can't hit a woman, but I'll beat that dirty bitch's ass for you!" she barked, getting hyped.

"She hiding out, sis, and that's why I need help finding her. There's only one person that I know of that will know how to find her, and Hajee is the only one that can get to this person for me," I told her.

"Let me guess... that dusty ass bitch Monica?" she asked, rolling her eyes.

"Yeah, but babe, if you ain't comfortable wit' it, I won't do it." Hajee jumped in. "We can find another way."

"How close will you have to be with her?" she asked, directing her question to him.

"Close enough to where she thinks that we not together no more," he admitted. "But like I said, if you ain't wit' it, I ain't wit' it," he threw in.

Shaking her head from side to side, she let out a sigh and ran her hand through her hair.

"No. You gotta do this. If it's the only way Key can get up wit' her, then you gotta do what you gotta do," she told him.

Letting go of the breath I didn't know I was holding, I smiled, relieved when she agreed to let him do it.

"You got a real one on ya team, bro. If he ever start fuckin' up again, Zoie, let a nigga know. It's about to get cold. Big nigga season is officially about to be in," Al told her, smiling.

"Get fucked up, Alphonse," Hajee warned.

"Say less, my nigga," Al told him.

"You ain't gotta tell me that I got a rider. My lil' mamas know what it is." Hajee smiled, pulling Zoie down into his lap.

"Long as you know. No fuckin', Hajee! I swear if you fuck this bitch again, I'm chopping your dick off. That's how we in the situation we in now. If you gotta kiss the bitch, you better give that hoe a peck and use dental dam or something," she told Hajee.

"Say less. I got you, ma." He smiled and kissed her. "Go 'head back in there wit' Moms before her nosy ass come back here."

"Okay." She agreed and kissed his cheek.

When she left the room, we talked for a few more seconds before trying to put together a way to lure Siya out, using Monica. I could tell Hajee didn't want no parts, but the lil' nigga would do anything for me, and I appreciated the hell out of him for that.

"Wait, you told Zoie that you was gon' put her ass in a full nelson. What the hell that is?" Al asked randomly.

"Oh, that's when you fucking her from the back, right, and you scoop your arms through her arms like this and rest them on the back of her head and put her ass in so she can't get loose. No running at all, and ain't got no choice but to take the dick," he explained, doing the gestures.

I couldn't do shit but laugh at these two fools, but I couldn't front and say I wasn't taking notes. Once we were done, we went back in the living room, and I kicked it with the family for an hour before heading home and preparing to cook for my girl. Em was doing something to a nigga, but I wasn't gon' flex and say I didn't like it. All I needed to do was handle this little bit of business I had in the streets, kill all my enemies, and we could live happily ever after. I had big plans for Em, and she didn't even know it yet, but she'd find out soon enough.

CHAPTER FIFTEEN

Zoie

My birthday was coming fast as hell and I was excited to finally be turning eighteen. With all the drama surrounding our lives, it was exciting to focus on something else other than how fucked up our lives really were.

River and O'Hajee were planning to throw my birthday party the same night as the grand opening to Myeke's new club called Pressure. Only thing I was allowed to know was that it was the night of my birthday, and I had to pick out the flavor cake I wanted. I was just happy to get a cake, hell. Brenda never celebrated my birthday with me, so just knowing I was going to be surrounded by the people that I loved, was enough for me.

Feeling a text come through on my phone, I looked down at it as I strolled through the mall with River.

My Heart: Checking in to say I love you and this shit will be over soon. It's killin' a nigga to be this far away from you but you got my heart and that's nothing but facts. Thank you for rockin' wit a nigga and daddy will be home before you know it. I'll talk to you soon.

Responding with a purple heart, I slid my phone back in my pocket. Between planning my birthday party, playing Monica close, and being in a fake relationship with her, Hajee barely had time to spend with me, and I hated it. I was the one that agreed to allow him to do it, but damn. If I knew it would be like this, I would've told his ass no in a heartbeat.

A part of me wanted to be selfish every day and tell him to bring his ass home and say fuck finding Myeke's baby mama, but I couldn't do him like that. He tried to act like it wasn't bothering him, but I knew being away from his child had to be hard. I was just happy that he had Em around to keep him distracted.

"Damn, trick. You didn't hear shit I said, did you?" River asked, snapping me out of my thoughts.

"No. I didn't. I got a text from Hajee, and it kind of threw me off," I admitted, looking over at her.

"How's that goin'?"

"It's going," I replied, shrugging my shoulders. "I can't say the shit isn't hard because he only comes home maybe twice a week and even then, he only stays for a few hours and has to head back to her. I want to be a bitch, but I understand why he's doing what he's doing."

"You're better than me, bitch, because there's no way in hell I would let my nigga play house wit' a hoe I know for a fact wants him. That, might I add, you caught him fuckin', and she claiming that she pregnant wit' his baby. That shit got 'dumb bitch' stamped all over it," she told me, shaking her head.

"Well damn, bitch, tell me how you really feel," I commented sarcastically, kissing my teeth.

"I'm just sayin', sis. That got shady written all over it. What makes you think, he ain't lovin' that shit and he ain't playin' both sides of the fence? I understand he doin' the shit for his brother, but how long does that shit take? They hood niggas; don't they just torture bitches for that type of information?"

"You watch too much TV, River. But I trust him. It may seem dumb, but I do. Regardless of the type of shit she on, I have to trust that he knows what he has in me and won't fuck that up for a bitch that he can tell means him no good. Besides, she's pregnant. If she wasn't, torture would've been on the top of my list," I told her.

"And again, I respect the fact that you trust O'Hajee. That nigga worships the ground you walk on. But my mama always said you never let ya man leave hungry or horny, and I know for a fact you're doing both. You still haven't gave it up, have you?"

She was right. I had healed up a while ago, but I couldn't go all the way with Hajee, even as much as I tried. I had started sucking his dick and would let him eat me out just to give him that sexual contact, but he needed more. I wasn't dumb. But every time we got ready to take it there, I would tense up and start crying hella hard. The shit was mad embarrassing, but he was always understanding.

"I try, River, but every time we about to have sex, flashes of that night come into my mind. Not to mention, I lost our baby because of it. Hajee would never pressure me for sex, but he's a man. He needs shit like that. Even when we don't," I admitted more to myself than to her.

"Look sis, I'm not tellin' you anything to make you doubt ya man, and you right, he should be understanding. You went through some fucked up shit, and even though I found out dumb late, I wouldn't want you to do anything that could possibly trigger those nightmares again. Have you thought about the counseling classes that Em offered?"

"No, because I'm not crazy!"

"Whoa, lil' mama, I never said you were," she said, holding her hands up in surrender. "How about we plan for you to do somethin' special for your birthday night? Everybody deserves a little birthday sex. After this party we gon' throw for you, you gon' wanna reward your man, sis. Trust me!"

"We can do that. Maybe I can do something sexy. Like get a lingerie piece?" I offered.

"Say no more. You know your friend got you. If I know nothin' else about life, I know about being a hoe!" she said, making me laugh.

"River, you are not a hoe."

"Girl, you ain't gotta lie to me. I'm okay wit' being a hoe. No strings attached, and I get my rocks off whenever I want it. Just like ol' girl Naya in the book I was just reading called *Philly's Finest* said, 'HOE IS LIFE!' Do you hear me, bih?" she asked, laughing, and I couldn't do anything but join in.

"You need help!" I laughed.

"And I plan to help myself to some dick as soon as this is over. So bring your practically married ass on so I can show you what you need to fuck your man's mind up," she told me, dragging me inside this lingerie store.

After spending damn near two hours inside, I ended up leaving with three separate lingerie sets, a teddy, the matching robe, the garters, and mask. I even let this bitch talk me into getting those sexy little heels with the fur on the toes. I had enough pieces to please him and keep him wanting more.

Before we left, I took a picture in the mirror of me in the all-white bra and panty set. I had the garter, robe, and matching heels on. Sending the picture to him, I smiled a little because I could imagine his face when he saw it.

Me: *When you pick out new outfits for daddy to rip off *smiley face**

My Heart: *Damn lil mamas. I'm glad you already know what's happenin'. That shit gon be destroyed fuckin' round wit me*

Me: *But baby I like this one *pouting face**

My Heart: *Shit me too mama. Gone head and grab two because I can't make no promises that it's gone survive*

Me: *Fine. I miss you and love you.*

My Heart: *Say less. It's almost over but nothing in this world is going to keep me away from you on your birthday.*

Me: *Promise?*

My Heart: *Nothing mama.*

Sliding my phone back in my pocket, I felt a little better after our brief interaction. I was praying that these next two weeks flew by because I was ready to have my man back with me full-time, but if Hajee hadn't gotten the information Myeke needed by then, I was willing to take things into my own hands, and I was sure no one wanted that.

* * *

After spending a couple more hours with River, I didn't feel like heading back to Manhattan to go home, so I decided to stop and grab some Kennedy Fried Chicken for me and Mama Tina.

"Can I get two chicken and fry plates, please, and two lemonades?" I asked.

After the cashier gave me my total, I paid for our food and sat in a booth and waited on the food to be ready. While I waited, I decided to play this game that O'Hajee had gotten me addicted to called *Word Mind*. It was mad addictive, and it made you think.

Halfway into my game, I heard arguing outside, causing me to look up and see what was going on. Looking up, my heart started beating inside my chest, and my mouth went dry. Dropping my phone on the table, I quickly broke my eyes away from the scene outside before standing to my feet, ready to leave.

This was Brooklyn, so I knew I would eventually see them, but I didn't expect to see them here. I had pushed all thoughts of my mom and Mike out of my head, but now that I saw them outside acting a fucking fool, all the stuff I tried to push to the back of my mind came rushing back, and I could feel my chest tightening up.

Just as I was walking out the door, the waitress called for me to come back because my food was ready. Going back to grab it, I thanked her and ducked down, trying not to be seen while I walked over to O'Hajee's car. He left it with me while he was with Monica because he knew that he could use her car anytime he wanted, and he didn't want me to be stranded at home.

Unlocking the car, I thought that I had gotten away until I heard my name being called and feet shuffling toward me.

"Zoie! Zoie! Hey you little light-skinned bitch! I know you hear me callin' you!" my mom shouted, causing a scene.

Turning around on my heels, I finally looked up as she was walking toward me, and she looked a hot ass mess. Her hair was matted all over her head, and she looked like she lost damn near fifty pounds in the last two months. I wanted to hate this woman with everything in me, but seeing her like this almost brought tears to my eyes. Until she opened her mouth and reminded me why I kept my distance from her.

"Oh, you too good for ya mama now? Huh? Is that it?" she asked when she was in arm's reach.

"What do you want, Brenda?" I questioned through gritted teeth.

"Brenda? You call me mama. I'm the one that pushed you out my pussy. No one else, you lil' whore, or did you forget that now that you gettin' a little dick that belongs to you," she said, and I had to look at her like she had lost her mind because I was convinced that she had.

"Excuse me?" I questioned.

"You heard me! You think you better than me because you fuckin' that lil' young boy wit' money, but you ain't shit. You the same lil' whore that sucked all my friends as a child just to make money. The same one that fucked my man and his friends!" she shouted. "You ain't shit. You can never turn your nose up at me! You are me!"

By now, a crowd of people had formed around and were shaking their heads at the shit that she was saying, and I could see the disgusted looks they had on their faces.

"You call pimpin' me out for fucking bottles, consensual? You let men touch and lick on me before I got my first period, just to satisfy your own desires. You're blaming me because your perverted ass boyfriend didn't rape me not once, but twice! You think I wanted this shit!" I yelled with tears in my eyes.

I was giving these people a show, but I didn't give a fuck. I couldn't believe the shit she was saying to me. Who the fuck is that damn twisted in the mind? Brenda and Mike, that's who.

"Oh, don't try to play so innocent. Mike told me you were begging for it," she had the nerve to say.

"And you believed him! I was fuckin' eleven! You heard me screaming and begging for them to stop. Begging you to make them stop, but you told them to keep me quiet! What kind of sick bitch watches her daughter get raped by three grown men and blames her for it! I swear to God if I had a gun, I'd blow your fuckin' brains out! You stupid, selfish bitch!" I screamed.

I was crying so hard and shaking so bad, I could barely see, and I hated that I let her see my tears. The smirk that she wore on her face let me know that this shit was getting her off, and that shit hurt more than anything. What had I ever done to her to make her hate me so much?

"You better be glad that's all I let them do to you. You've been living with me rent free for too long. Walkin' around like the Queen of Sheba. I'm glad they knocked your ass off that pedestal," she scoffed.

"I'M SEVENTEEN! YOU'RE MY MOTHER! IT'S YOUR

FUCKIN' JOB!"

"Come on, ma. You don't gotta listen to this shit," I heard someone say, trying to pull me away.

"Why? Why couldn't you just be normal? Why couldn't you just protect me?" I asked through tears, breaking down.

"Come on," the guy said again, and I let him guide me back toward my car.

Feeling a pair of eyes on me, I looked up and locked eyes with Mike, and his ass wore the same sick smirk that my mom did. The guy must've felt me tense because before I could get to him to wipe the smirk off his face, the guy was dragging me away.

"YOU SICK BASTARD! YOU RUINED MY LIFE! ALL THIS SHIT IS YOUR FAULT! IF IT'S THE LAST THING I DO, I WILL KILL YOU! I WILL KILL YOU BOTH!" I screamed and fought against the guy until he was able to get me to my car and put me inside.

As soon as my butt hit the seat, I banged my hands on the steering wheel and started crying harder. I can't believe after all the shit that she did to me, I still let her get to me.

"You alright?" I heard the guy ask, and for the first time, I looked up at him.

He was the epitome of fine. He stood about six feet four of nothing but muscle. He was the color of chocolate but I could tell that he wasn't all the way black because of his features. I wasn't sure what he was mixed with but whatever it was worked for him. And oh gawd, his beard was LIFE!

"I'm fine. Thank you," I told him, trying to calm down my breathing.

"No problem. You too fine to be lettin' shit like that get to you. Just say the word, and their asses will be a distant memory," he told me.

"Thank you for that, but that's somethin' that I will have to deal wit' on my own."

"I respect it. Maybe I can take you out or somethin'," he offered.

"You must not be from 'round here?"

"Is it that obvious?"

"Your accent sticks out like a sore thumb," I admitted as I laughed, wiping my tears.

"She smiles. I swear you a sexy lil' jawn," he complimented me. "But I'm from across the bridge. Philly actually."

"Oh. Well thank you…"

"Deuce. Nice to meet you." He introduced himself.

"Zoie. Nice to meet you," I said, shaking his hand. "But like I was sayin', thank you for everything, but I have a boyfriend."

"That's a lucky nigga. But here, take my number. If you change your mind about ya lil' problem, you know who to call."

"I'on know. My nigga a lil' crazy."

"And I'm psycho, baby. I ain't on no funny shit, I swear. Gimme ya phone," he told me, but didn't wait for me to hand it to him before sliding it out my hand and facing it towards me so I could unlock it.

Once I did, he locked his number in and handed it back to me.

"Now, you can hit me up when you up to it. No pressure. Just in case." He smiled.

"Just in case," I repeated. "Let me get out of here. This food is probably ice cold now, and I'm tired of people looking at me like I'm a freak in a circus."

"Say less, ma. Get home safe and remember what I said," he told me before walking away and swaggering back across the street.

I watched him until he got in his car and drove off. I didn't know why, but something told me that Deuce was more trouble than he was worth, and I loved my man, so I could never see myself stepping out on him, but if I needed someone to help me with my problem, I definitely knew who to call.

CHAPTER SIXTEEN

O'Hajee

I had been playing Monica close for weeks and she was starting to think this shit was something that it wasn't. I missed my girl like crazy, and I had to play my part to a tee, but this shit was starting to get to be too damn much. The moment Monica started talking about us moving into a bigger house and baby names, I knew it was time for me to get what I came here for and get the fuck on.

I had taken notice that she had been ducking out at least twice a day, taking private phone calls, but I never called her out on it. It could be a nigga for all I knew, but there was something telling me that everything I needed and wanted was in her phone.

Rolling over in the bed, I realized she was still sleep. Her phone kept going off on the nightstand. Easing out the bed, careful not to wake her, I slid it off the table and went to the bathroom. Pressing the home button, I noticed she didn't have a code on her phone, making my job that much easier.

Clicking her messages, I saw that she had four unopened text messages from an unsaved number. Opening the messages, I scrolled

169

up to see who the text messages were from.

Unknown: Damn bitch. Take Hajee's dick out your mouth long enough to respond to my messages.

Unknown: Helloooo! Bih! I know you saw my text!

Unknown: Ugh call me or text back or somethin'! This shit is important!

Unknown: Monica! If you do not answer my text, I'ma file a missing person's report on your ass.

Studying the way Monica texted, I sat down on the toilet seat and started to text the person back.

Me: Sorry girl. You know my baby daddy had me dead to the world.

Unknown: Thank God! I thought he found something out. Have you found out anything else about Myeke and his bitch?

Me: No not yet. You know that nigga closed lip about his family.

Unknown: Well we got to do somethin' and fast. I leave to go back to Georgia tomorrow and we need to put our plan in motion. Like today.

Plan? What fucking plan? I thought to myself.

Thinking fast on my feet, I smiled to myself before sending her a text. I knew exactly how to get both these bitches in one place.

Me: Hajee don't know I heard him but he got some type of grand opening thing to go to tonight for Key new club. I'll send you the address and we can put the plan in motion then.

Unknown: Good! We can kill two birds with one stone! Don't forget!

Me: I won't. He gettin' suspicious. Don't text me back. I'll see you tonight.

Unknown: Okay bet.

After sending her the address, I deleted the messages between us as well as the messages that Siya sent her before. I made sure that I covered my tracks before going back in the room and setting her phone back in its original spot.

Sliding back in the bed, I sent a group text to Al and Myeke to let them know that everything was a go. It was after two in the morning, so I wasn't expecting them to text back until later on.

Exiting out of my message with them, I clicked my message thread with Zoie and sent my baby a message.

Me: Happy Birthday baby! You finally legal. Oh shit lil nigga, I see you lol. I'm sorry I'm not there to bring it in with you but I got you tonight. I'm ending all this shit tonight. Daddy coming home to you. I'll see you in a few hours. Enjoy the day I have planned out for you. You deserve it and so much more. I love you.

Before I could put my phone back down, an incoming text came in from her.

My Everything: Thank you baby! I'm so ready to be back in your arms. I will see you tonight and I love you too!

Me: Bet.

Closing out the screen, I rolled on my back and stared at the ceiling, finally feeling at ease about the shit that I was doing. I saw that Siya was on that good bullshit and she had to go; tonight had to go off without a hitch. If Monica got in the way or became a problem, her ass could definitely get it too.

I was tired of being the nice Hajee because motherfuckas thought that I was soft. They were about to find out that fucking with my family and my girl were off limits. Closing my eyes with a smile on my face, a calm settled over me, and I could already tell that today was going to be a good day.

* * *

Getting up a few hours later, I rolled over and realized that Monica had already gotten out the bed. Getting out the bed, I went to handle my hygiene and got dressed before going down the stairs to find her.

As soon as I opened the room door, I smelled food, and a nigga's stomach instantly started talking to me. Walking into the kitchen, I watched her do a little dance while she fixed breakfast; slim, chocolate, and she could have any man she wanted. Only problem was she couldn't have me. Maybe in another life, but not this one. Letting my eyes roam over her body, they stopped at her stomach, and I could see a slight bump forming. It wasn't big, and if I didn't know she was pregnant, I'd swear she was just full.

Clearing my throat, I made my presence known in the kitchen before walking all the way inside and taking a seat at the bar.

"Good morning! How'd you sleep?" she asked, smiling.

"Pretty good. I can't complain," I replied, taking a strip of bacon and biting it.

"That's good. What do you got planned for today? I see you already dressed and ready to go, and it isn't even ten yet."

"I got some running around to do, but I want to ask you something."

"Oh yeah? What's that?" she asked, bringing a plate of food over and setting it on the bar in front of me.

Pausing momentarily, I said my grace before opening my eyes back up and pouring syrup on my pancakes.

"Myeke's opening a club, and tonight is the grand opening. I was seeing if you wanted to be my date."

"Really? Aww, baby, I'd love to!" She squealed, jumping up and down.

"Good. I'ma leave you a couple dollars to go grab you something to wear. The party is white, red, and black. The only person gon' be wearing black is the guest of honor. Women wear red and men wear white," I explained.

"I already have the perfect outfit in mind. I been dying to wear these booties I got months ago, and this is the perfect chance to wear them out."

"Okay, cool. Well, I'ma leave you to it. I'll text you the address a little later. I'll be out the house all day, so just meet me there."

"Okay, baby!" she answered before running up the stairs.

After I finished eating my food, I dug into my pocket and put three thousand on the bar before snatching up the keys and heading out the door. I made a mental note to have one of Myeke's runners bring the car back over. I had plans on riding out with him and Al since River was bringing Zoie to the club later on tonight.

For the next few hours, I ran around the city making sure everything was perfect. I needed everything to go off without a hitch so I could be laid up underneath my girl at the end of the night. Once I got the confirmation from River that she had Zoie and she would make sure her birthday went as planned, I headed to Pressure to make sure that they had got the decorations perfect. I was trying to get some pussy tonight, and nothing was gonna stop me.

Myeke

"Baby, do you have to go?" Em whined, rolling over in the bed, wrapped up in the covers.

"Yes, I gotta make sure that everything is in order for the club. Besides, you gotta get up anyway to get your outfit. Zoie and River supposed to be here to get you in like an hour," I said, watching her pout.

"I don't wanna."

"Girl, get ya spoiled ass up," I said, smacking her on her ass.

"Ouch! Nobody told you to fuck me into submission last night. I could've been up hours ago," she pointed out.

"And nobody told your ass to be walkin' around the crib in them lil' ass shorts. I already told your ass to dress like a nun when you around me."

"I don't have a nun costume, Myeke."

"Well then, you always gon' get touched," I replied with a shrug.

Ever since that first night we fucked, I couldn't get enough of Emily or her pussy. Her walls fit me like a glove, and every time I slid in it, I swear I wanted to nut instantly. It didn't matter where we were; if I got turned on, I was fucking my girl, and I dared her to tell me that we couldn't. I would behave then, but the moment we got home, shit was on and popping.

She basically moved in my crib, and having her here made it feel like a home, but the only thing missing was my little man. I had been driving myself crazy trying to hunt down Siya since the day she popped up on Em at the hospital. I had Hajee getting close to Monica's ass, but she wasn't mentioning Siya at all. I was happy as hell when I woke up to the text he sent me saying that everything was ending tonight.

That had to mean that either Monica finally slipped up or he finally found something that could help us out. Either way, I was one step closer to getting my hands on this bitch and getting my son. I hadn't forgot about Deuce's bitch ass either, but the streets were all quiet when it came to that nigga.

He must've had Houdini blood running through his veins because he was ghost for real. He vanished out of thin air, but just like Siya's ass, he would have to resurface eventually. When he finally did, I was gon' be waiting on his ass with bells on.

"Girl, you better get out the bed or I'm gettin' back in," I warned Em.

Jumping out of the bed almost immediately, she swung her legs over the side of the bed and made a beeline to the bathroom connected to my bedroom.

"Oh no. I need my uterus today," she said as she walked past me.

"I thought that shit would make you change your mind."

"Fuck you!" she shouted through the bathroom door.

Shaking my head, I finished getting dressed just as a text from

O'Hajee came through for me to open the front door. Taking the steps two at a time, I headed to the front door and unlocked it, letting his ass inside.

"What's good, youngin?" I greeted.

"I can't call it," he replied. "Oh, I need you to call one of your runners to take the car back to Monica. I invited her tonight, and I need to make sure she can get there on her own so I can spend time with Zoie," he said.

Spinning around, I looked at the nigga like he had an arm growing out of his forehead.

"What the hell would possess you to invite the girl that think she's yo' main bitch, to your girl birthday party? I understand that we pretending, but that shit liable to cause some real-life issues," I told him, shaking my head.

"Let me handle this. When you find out why, you gon' be ready to kiss a nigga," he commented, sitting down on the couch in my living room.

"I'on know about all that gay shit, but I'm eager as hell to figure out how you plan to pull this shit off. You can't keep them from bumping into each other all night."

"Yes I can, because I plan to put Monica in a VIP. Right along wit' Siya," he revealed.

"Siya?" I asked.

Now my interest was definitely piqued. How the fuck did he manage to find her?

"Yep. Monica's phone kept blowing up early this morning, and it woke me up out my sleep, so on some fuck nigga shit, I decided to check her phone, and I'm glad I did. I had already had the feeling that everything I needed was in her phone, and I was right."

"Bro. What the fuck? That's all you gon' say, my nigga?" I asked.

"Chill out. So, I open the messages and see they're all from this unsaved number, and so I opened it up and read the messages and confirmed that they were from Siya. It took me a second to figure out the way that Monica texted, but when I did, I started texting Siya, pretending to be her and invited her to the grand opening tonight," he told me.

"And that shit worked?"

"Like a charm. Before I deleted the messages, I sent her the address and told her don't call or text for the rest of the day because I was becoming suspicious of all the secret phone calls and hidden text messages. She agreed, and I haven't heard shit else since.

This morning, I woke up, invited Monica to the party, then broke her off with some bread for her to grab something to wear. They apparently got something planned. She texted Monica and said that she was leaving for Georgia tomorrow, and whatever they planned had to be done tonight. I figured why not have everything go down at the club. That way, we can control the outcome."

Nodding my head in approval, I had to admit that the shit was genius, and if he was able to keep Monica and Zoie from seeing each other, then we would pull it off. I could grab Siya before she even realized what happened and have Al escort Monica out before Zoie noticed her in the building. The shit was perfect.

"Look at you using your brain and shit. I knew you didn't have that big motherfucka for nothing," I joked.

"Yeah, aight, my nigga. Just say you proud of a nigga, and we can make sure that we end this shit tonight," he told me.

"I am proud of you, Haj," I told him, getting serious. "And I appreciate you putting your personal shit to the side to help me out. You got shit with Zoie that you need to be tying up, but instead, you making sure that I'm good and in one piece. I can't thank you enough."

"Say less." He nodded. "That's what brothers are for. Don't worry; the shit with Zoie and her people is in the works. I just been waiting for the right time to handle it. She been in a good head space, and I don't want to kick up dirt, you know what I'm saying?"

"I feel you. Well, let's get out of here and make sure everything is in order. We got a long night ahead," I told him.

"Ok, bet."

After I told Em that I would see her later on tonight, I sent out the text to my runners to make sure they came to pick up Monica's car and made sure that Al had everything set before heading back over to the club with Hajee to make sure to get dressed.

I was so hyped that a nigga was bouncing up and down like a kid in a candy store. The thoughts of getting my hands on this bitch made my mouth water, and I could just taste the victory. Yeah, today had definitely been a good day, but tonight was going to be better.

Zoie

It's my motherfucking birthday, bihh! I was finally legal, and couldn't no one tell me nothing. I had been ripping and running around all day with River and Em, getting ready for tonight, and it was finally time to see what all the secrecy was about.

O'Hajee and Myeke had outdone themselves. They sent the three of us out to pick out our outfits for the night, mani/pedis, and to the hair salon to get slayed. My normal curly hair was bone straight, and my face was beat to perfection. Everyone else was supposed to wear red and white, but O'Hajee specifically told River that I had to wear black. I wasn't complaining, because the black dress I picked out was to die for.

The dress went on like a bodysuit and nothing covered my legs in the front. The back part of the dress was sheer and followed behind me like the train of a wedding dress. The neckline made my little bitty titties look bigger, and the black spiked toy red bottoms that I paired with the outfit put it over the top. I was looking sexy and feeling even better.

"Yasss, that's my bih right there! Girl, Hajee is going to have a fuckin' heart attack. Do you hear me, sis?" River asked, coming into the room fully dressed.

She rocked an all red two-piece jumpsuit with thigh high nude boots. Instead of the bottom half being pants, they were shorts that cuffed her ass perfectly. Every time she walked, her ass jiggled to a beat of its own. She had her hair styled in this sexy ass blonde asymmetrical bob, and the color reminded me of Ronnie off *Player's Club*.

"I know you ain't talking the way your ass is poking out the bottom of them shorts." I laughed, tugging on them jokingly.

"Yeah, she right, River. Give me some of that ass," Em joked, putting her gold choker on her neck.

Em's red dress seemed simple when she was approaching you, minus the way her titties were sitting up in it and the slit that ran up the side. But babayyyee, when she turned around, there was no back to the dress. The whole back was out, and it literally started again at the crack of her ass.

When Myeke saw her, he was going to say fuck the party and have that dress on the floor while he fucked the shit out of her in his office.

"We all look fine, okay! All I know is, while y'all get in trouble and y'all men make y'all sit down, just know that I'm gon' be shaking these cheeks in the middle of the dance floor," River told us, laughing.

"Don't worry. Someone gon' tie your ass down one of these days." Em said as she laughed.

"Uh-uh. Don't wish that evil on me." River gasped, pretending to be offended. "Z, tell ya girl what it is when it comes to me. Say it one time for the people in the back."

"HOE IS LIFE!" we yelled in unison before falling over laughing.

"Let's take a couple pictures so we can get out of here. We already over thirty minutes out, and if O'Hajee text me one more time askin' me if we're on our way, I'm goin' to fuck your man up, sis," River said.

"Leave my baby alone. He just ready to see his lil' mamas." I blushed.

"Yeah, whatever, hoe. He needs to be callin' you then," she joked.

"Oh, whatever. Come on and take the pictures so I can go see what my man has in store for me."

"Then what the fuck am I, chopped liver? I had something to do wit' this planning to!"

"But am I fuckin' you?" I asked.

"Touché, bitch. Touché."

Taking a few pictures, we picked the ones we liked before uploading them to our IG and Facebook pages. We were on one the whole way to the club. O'Hajee decided at the last minute that it would be better to get us a party bus, and we were lit. It was only the three of us on there, but you couldn't tell us we weren't in the club.

There were so many bottles of alcohol, that we were tipsy as fuck by the time we made it to the club, and not to mention high. I don't know where River stashed that blunt of sour, but the shit had me mellow.

New York had the best sour on Earth, and no one could tell me different. When we pulled up to *Pressure*, the line was damn near down the block, and I was happy that I didn't have to wait in that long ass line with the rest of them.

"Wait, bitch! I almost forgot," River said, handing me an iced out gold crown.

"I can't wear this. Someone is goin' to rob me," I told her, trying to hand it back.

"Myeke is your brother-in-law, and O'Hajee is your man. Who would be dumb enough to try to rob you, Zoie?" Em asked me.

"Facts," was all I said before putting the crown on my head and looking at them for approval.

When they nodded and started smiling, I knew that meant I was on point.

"Okay, bitches! Let the festivities begin!" River yelled as the doors of the party bus opened and we stepped out.

We could hear the catcalls of thirsty niggas instantly, as well as the chorus of hating bitches sucking their teeth. River was busy texting on her phone as we made our way to the door. Just as I was about to tell them who I was, Al stepped out and told the bouncer to let us past.

"Damn he fine," I heard River mumble, and I didn't have to look to see she was talking about Al.

Al was a big dude, but he wasn't sloppy. He just looked like he lived in the gym, and his tatted skin and tapered fade set off his look.

"What's up, birthday girl?" he greeted, bending down and pulling me into a hug. "What's up, sis?" he said to Em, when he let me go, before hugging her and turning to River.

I was shocked because normally River was all mouth, but now she was standing here speechless while she looked at Al like she wanted to ride his face in the middle of the club.

"Al. But you can call me Alphonse," he told her, reaching his hand out to shake hers.

"River," was all she could say as she tried to break out of the trance that he had her in.

"Nice to meet you. Come on, ladies. The fellas waiting on y'all," he said, smirking at River who was still looking at him.

"Sis, are you okay?" I had to ask when we started walking.

"Who is he?" she asked, completely ignoring my question.

"I thought you knew everything. That's Myeke's right-hand man, Al," I said.

"I will gladly turn in my hoe card for him. That man is all types of fine."

"You stupid." I laughed.

"But I'm so serious," she replied.

"Y'all wait right here. I'ma go get the guys," Al told us, leaving us at the bar.

"You guys want something to drink?" Em shouted over the music.

"Get me a blue motherfucker, please!" River yelled.

"Just give me whatever. We know I don't know nothing about alcohol," I told her and she agreed before moving behind us to get the bartender's attention.

Young Thug's hit song "Best Friend" came on, and River wasted no time grabbing my hand and dragging me through the crowd to the middle of the dance floor.

Normally, I was shy, but with the amount of alcohol in my system and the weed that I had coursing through my body, all that shit went out the window as I started twerking to the beat.

"Yassss, bihhhh!" River yelled over the music, egging me on. "That's my best friend. That's my best friend."

I was fucking it up while River smacked my ass until the deejay switched to "Freak Hoe" by Speaker Knockers, and it was my turn to be River's hype man.

"Fuck it up, bih!" I yelled, smacking her on the butt.

"Can you do all that on me?" I heard a deep voice ask in my ear as they snaked their arm around my waist.

Spinning on my heels, I was ready to dog someone out until I realized who it was and broke out into a full-blown smile.

"Deuce! Oh my gosh, what are you doing here!" I squealed, giving him a hug.

"I couldn't miss the hottest party everyone been talkin' about for weeks. What about you? You breaking dress code and shit. You the only one in this jawn wearin' black," he pointed out.

The way he was eyeing my body, I was glad that it was dark in here or he would see how red my cheeks were under his gaze.

"This is my party!" I revealed. "Well, that and my brother in law's grand opening," I added.

"Your brother-in-law?"

"Yeah! You may know him. His name is Myeke. He a big deal over in East New York," I told him, smiling.

"Oh yeah! I've heard the name. What you doin' after this?" he asked, whispering in my ear.

"I'm not sure."

"Well you got my number. Use it," he flirted.

"I may do that, but I won't make any promises," I told him.

"Yo, Z! The guys are waiting for us by the bar!" River yelled in my ear.

"Okay, here I come," I responded before turning around to tell Deuce I would see him later, but he had already disappeared into the crowd.

Shrugging it off, I went back to where we left Em at the bar to see Myeke and Al standing with her.

"Happy birthday, lil' sis!" Myeke yelled the moment he saw me.

"Thank you, brah! This party is mad crazy. It's dope as hell!" I yelled in his ear.

"No problem. You know a nigga name brings the whole city out," he joked.

"Say less!" I smiled. "Where's your brother at?" I asked when I didn't notice him.

"He around here somewhere," he responded but didn't look me in my eyes.

Ignoring his comment, I decided to scan the crowd so that I could go find my man. I missed him, and I understood he was busy, but I just wanted to put my eyes on him. It didn't take long for my eyes to land on him, and when they did, I broke out into a smile. My baby was looking sexy as hell in his all white.

"River, I'll be right back. I found Hajee. I'm about to go get him!" I yelled in her ear.

"Okay, sis!" she replied.

Walking through the crowd, I started to make my way to my man with my smile still dancing on my lips, but by the time I was within a hundred feet of him, the smile fell from my face.

I watched in horror as he whispered in Monica's ear while she had a smile plastered on her face. He was rubbing on her exposed thigh, and whatever he was saying must've sounded good because she looked like she was about to cum in her panties.

O'Hajee must've felt my presence because he looked up and locked eyes with me. I could see him pleading with his eyes, and I saw his mouth open to call me, but I moved away through the crowd before he could come towards me.

How the fuck could I be so fucking stupid? River was right. He was doing me dirty even after the first time I forgave him. I could feel myself getting ready to break down, and I thought about going to the bathroom to calm down, but the line was too long, and I didn't need these nosy ass bitches in my business.

Feeling myself getting overwhelmed, I leaned against the wall in a corner and closed my eyes, trying to get my breathing under control so I wouldn't cry.

"You good, ma? I was headed to the bathroom, and saw you standing here looking like you about to break down. You good?" Deuce asked, seeming to pop out of thin air.

"No. I just want to get out of here. I need fresh air," I told him.

"Okay, let me walk you," he offered.

"No, it's okay. I don't want my boyfriend to come looking for me and you be around. That wouldn't be pretty."

"Shorty, I already told you I ain't worried about ya mans. Let me just make sure you get in and out good, and I swear I'll leave you alone," he said.

Thinking it over for a few seconds, I finally agreed before leaning off the wall and stumbling.

"You sure you good?" he asked, concerned.

"Yeah. I just had a few drinks."

"I see. Here I just got me a bottle of water from the bar. I opened it, but I haven't drunk out of it yet," he said, handing me the bottle of water.

"Thank you."

"No problem. Come on so we can get you some fresh air so you can sober up," he said, leading me back toward the crowd.

"No, wait! I don't want to go that way. I don't want my boyfriend to see me," I said.

"Okay. There's a side exit this way," he told me and held my hand.

Stepping outside into the night air, I closed my eyes and took a gulp out of the water. I damn near drank half the bottle before I stopped. The alcohol and weed had my mouth hella dry, and the water was exactly what I needed.

Leaning my back against the wall, I closed my eyes again and tried to calm myself down. My heart started to beat fast and my legs started to get weak.

"Zoie? You good?" I heard Deuce's muffled voice.

"I don'ttt… I don't feel so gooodd," I slurred, opening my eyes.

I could feel my legs giving out on me as one of the Deuce's standing in front of me scooped me in their arms. Fading in and out of consciousness, I felt like I was floating through the air.

"Don't worry; I'ma take good care of you," Deuce told me, sliding me into the passenger seat of a car.

My vision was so blurred that I couldn't focus on anything, and the fogginess of my brain was becoming too much to fight through.

"Just sit back and ride," was the last thing I heard before the darkness took me whole.

TO BE CONTINUED…

NOTE FROM THE AUTHOR

I want to thank you for reading this book. I swear I love you from the bottom of my heart and you make this journey worth it. Please leave me a review to let me know what you think. I'm always looking for feedback. The next book is coming very SOON; a lot sooner than you think (smile), but make sure you subscribe to my email list to get first look at cover reveals, sneak peeks, and release dates for upcoming releases. Thank you again, and trust you will hear from me soon.

Porschea Jade

ACKNOWLEDGMENTS

Girls, everything that mommy does, she does it to make you proud and to better your future. I strive to show you that you can be better than your circumstance because I became so much more than anyone thought I would be. Alani, Elizabeth, Amelia, and Paisley, just know that you all give me purpose. I love you to the death of me.

Kiara, you already know that you are my biggest supporter, and you've shown me time and time again that when it us or the world, you'll choose us every time. You're my sister, but you're also my best friend. My little sister harder than most of you... well, you know the rest. LOL. I love you to the moon and back. We almost there, love. Nowhere to go but up from here.

Shontea! I want to thank you from the bottom of my heart! When I say you are one of the dopest people I know, I kid you not! You have been rocking with me since the very first book I submitted, and you still going strong. I annoy you, but it's all love. We ain't going nowhere but up from here, and I already know that you're down for the ride.

Tay Nasty! When I say you are the truth, boo, I mean it. You have been making sure I stay focused and pushing me just as much I push you. I don't call it micromanaging when your friends want to see you good. That's friendship. You can call me a drill sergeant all you want to, but it works for us, so we gon' keep going! 2018 is OURS! Believe that!

Law! Girl, when I say you stress me out, I kid you not. You are one of the toughest test readers I have right now, and you are the true book plug! You rocking with the kid, and I swear I appreciate every piece of advice you give me and all the feedback I receive. You the truth, ma!

To the readers that I gained from *Something About the Hood in Him*, I want to thank you from the bottom of my heart for taking a chance on me. Y'all make all of this worthwhile. If you heard about me due to *The Vendetti Family: Money, Murder, Mayhem*, then I thank you as well. And even for the ones that are picking up this one right here, I thank you as well. You guys make the long days, sleepless nights, and tired days, worth it. I hope y'all enjoy this book as much as I enjoyed writing it. I fall in love with all my characters, and I hope you will too. Don't forget to leave me a review and let me know what you think! My inbox is always open.

Porschea Jade

CONNECT WITH ME ON SOCIAL MEDIA TO GET TO KNOW THE WRITER BEHIND THE PEN.

Facebook: Porschea Jade

Twitter: @IAmPorscheaJade

Snapchat: simply_porschea

IG: Simplyy_porscheajade

Periscope: @iamporscheajade

Facebook readers group: Porschea Jade's Urban Exscape

BOOKS BY PORSCHEA JADE:

Something About the Hood in Him (standalone)

The Vendetti Family: Money, Murder, & Mayhem

The Vendetti Family 2: Money, Murder, & Mayhem (the finale)

The Love a Boss Gives (standalone)

I'd Rather Be Ya Hitta: Finding Love in Little Havana

I'd Rather Be Ya Hitta: Finding Love in Little Havana 2

Jackboys and The Women They Love

He's a Different Kind of Hood:
(Something About the Hood in Him Spinoff) 1 & 2

Good Girl with a Dope Boy Fetish

Looking for a publishing home?

Royalty Publishing House, Where the Royals reside, is accepting submissions for writers in the urban fiction genre. If you're interested, submit the first 3-4 chapters with your synopsis to submissions@royaltypublishinghouse.com.

Check out our website for more information: www.royaltypublishinghouse.com.

Text ROYALTY to 42828 to join our mailing list!

To submit a manuscript for our review, email us at
submissions@royaltypublishinghouse.com

Text RPHCHRISTIAN to 22828 for our
CHRISTIAN ROMANCE novels!

Text RPHROMANCE to 22828 for our
INTERRACIAL ROMANCE novels!

Get LiT!

Download the LiT eReader app today and enjoy exclusive content, free books, and more

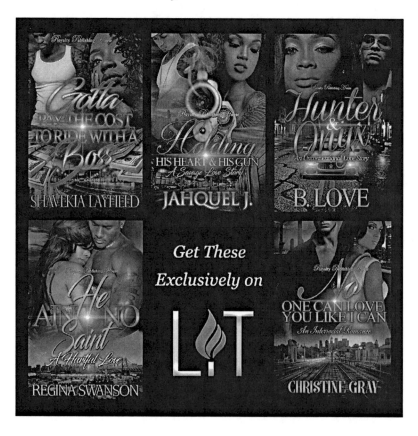

Do You Like CELEBRITY GOSSIP?

Check Out QUEEN DYNASTY!
Visit Our Site: www.thequeendynasty.com

CPSIA information can be obtained
at www.ICGtesting.com
Printed in the USA
LVOW10s0107231217
560596LV00015B/1064/P